MERLIN'S DRAGON

DRAGON

ULTIMATE MAGIC

T. A. BARRON

MERLIN'S DRAGON

BOOK 3
ULTIMATE MAGIC

PHILOMEL BOOKS

AN IMPRINT OF PENGUIN GROUP (USA) INC.

Patricia Lee Gauch, Editor

PHILOMEL BOOKS

A division of Penguin Young Readers Group.
Published by The Penguin Group.
Penguin Group (USA) Inc., 375 Hudson Street, New York, NY 10014, U.S.A.
Penguin Group (Canada), 90 Eglinton Avenue East, Suite 700, Toronto, Ontario
M4P 2Y3, Canada (a division of Pearson Penguin Canada Inc.).
Penguin Books Ltd, 80 Strand, London WC2R 0RL, England.
Penguin Ireland, 25 St. Stephen's Green, Dublin 2, Ireland
(a division of Penguin Books Ltd).
Penguin Group (Australia), 250 Camberwell Road, Camberwell, Victoria 3124,
Australia (a division of Pearson Australia Group Pty Ltd).
Penguin Books India Pvt Ltd, 11 Community Centre, Panchsheel Park,
New Delhi—110 017, India.
Penguin Group (NZ), 67 Apollo Drive, Rosedale, North Shore 0632, New Zealand
(a division of Pearson New Zealand Ltd).
Penguin Books (South Africa) (Pty) Ltd, 24 Sturdee Avenue, Rosebank,
Johannesburg 2196, South Africa.
Penguin Books Ltd, Registered Offices: 80 Strand, London WC2R 0RL, England.

Published simultaneously in Canada.   Printed in the United States of America.
Design by Semadar Megged.   Text set in ITC Galliard.

Library of Congress Cataloging-in-Publication Data
Barron, T. A.
Merlin's dragon. Book three, Ultimate magic / T. A. Barron.
p. cm.
Summary: The dragon Basilgarrad leads the ultimate battle to save the land of
Avalon, and, finally, must decide whether to obey his dear friend Merlin's request,
even though it means giving up his powers as a warrior.
[1. Dragons—Fiction. 2. Magic—Fiction. 3. Fantasy.] I. Title.
II. Title: Ultimate magic.
PZ7.B27567Mfn 2010
[Fic]—dc22   2009041645

ISBN 978-0-399-25217-4
1   3   5   7   9   10   8   6   4   2

Dedicated to

Anne Schieckel, Lisette Buchholz, and Irmela Brender—

who have done so much, with great skill and passion,

to bring my stories to German readers

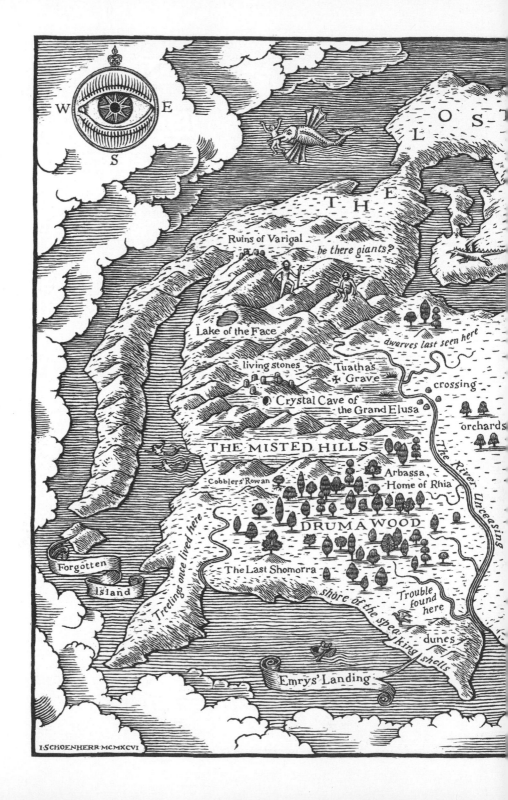

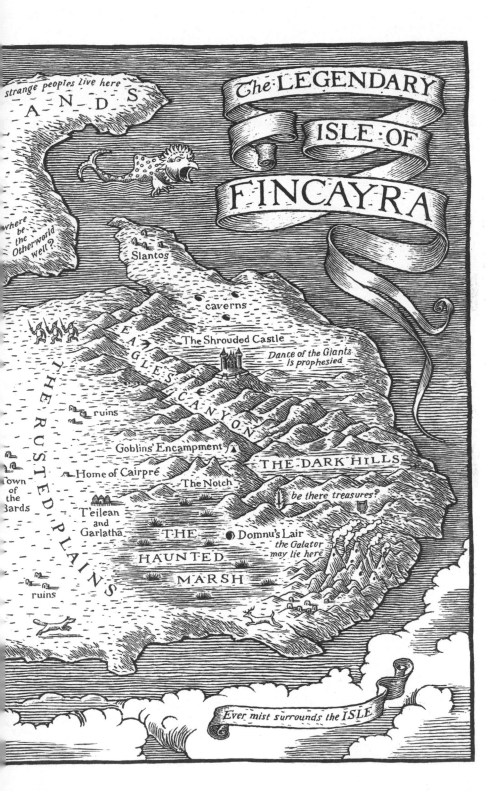

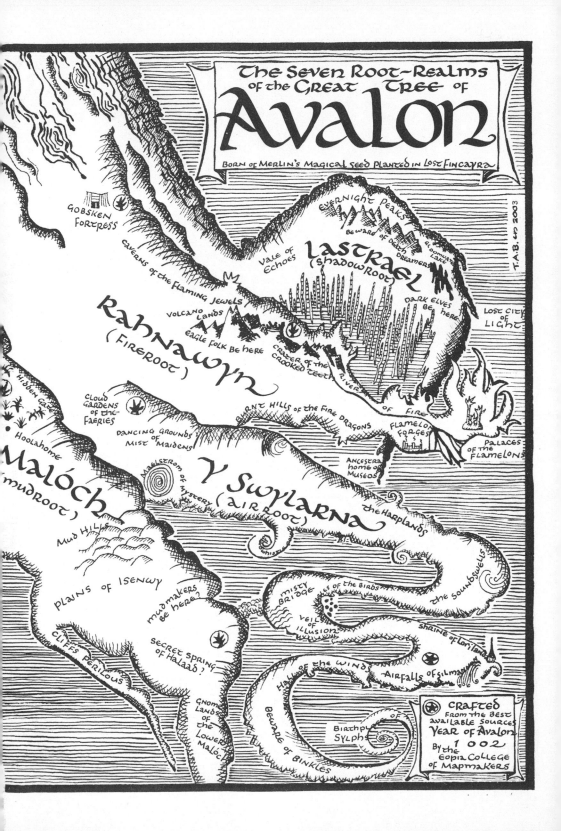

The Seven Root-Realms of the GREAT TREE of

Avalon

BORN of MERLIN's Magical SEED Planted in Lost FINCAYRA

T.A.B. HD 2003

GOBSKEN FORTRESS

EVERNIGHT PEAKS

Beware of Death Dreamers

BLOODNOOT LAKE

Vale of Echoes

CAVERNS of the FLAMING JEWELS

lastrael
(Shadowroot)

DARK ELVES BE HERE

LOST CITY of LIGHT

VOLCANO LANDS

Rahnawyn
(FIREROOT)

EAGLE FOLK BE HERE

CRATER of the CROOKED TEETH

RIVER of FIRE

Hidden Cave

CLOUD GARDENS of the FAERIES

BURNT HILLS of the FIRE DRAGONS

FLAMELON FORGES

PALACES of the FLAMELONS

Hoolahome

DANCING GROUNDS of MIST MAIDENS

ANCESTRAL HOME of MUSEOS

Malóch
(mudroot)

MAELSTROM of MYSTERY

Y Swylarna
(AIR ROOT)

the HARPLANDS

MUD HILLS

PLAINS OF ISENWY

MUDMAKERS BE HERE?

MISTY BRIDGE

ES of the BIRDS

the SOUNDSWELLS

VEIL of ILLUSION

SHRINE of LORILANDA

CLIFFS PERILOUS

SECRET SPRING of HALAAD?

HALL of the WINDS

AIRFALLS of SILMAWN

GNOME LAND of the LOWER MALÓC

BEWARE of BINKLES

BIRTHPL of SYLPHS

CRAFTED FROM the BEST available SOURCES YEAR of Avalon 1 002 By the EOPIA COLLEGE of Mapmakers

CONTENTS

Merlin's Dragon

Dragon

Ultimate Magic

PROLOGUE

For a big surprise, I look for a small mystery.

Basilgarrad lifted his enormous head, scanning the rolling meadows that reached to the distant trees. His dragon's eyes glittered as his powerful shoulder muscles tensed. Both of his furled wings—each one big enough to hold the entire body of a normal-sized dragon—shook with anticipation, their bony tips clattering against the scales of his back.

A breeze suddenly stirred, bending the blades of grass around him. To his own surprise, he caught some of his favorite scents. Dank woodland mushrooms. Cedar resins, both sharp and sweet. Tangy apples, so ready for eating they would almost peel themselves in a young elf's hands. Enchanted spiderwebs, sturdy enough to hold a boulder. Fresh spray from the headwaters of the River Relentless.

For an instant, taking in those rich aromas, he remembered why he treasured this realm, this world of so much life. So much magic. And why, if necessary, he would die to protect it.

His gargantuan tail, ending with a massive club, slammed against the ground. Tremors shot in all directions, cracking open crevasses in the meadows and shaking the faraway trees. For he had smelled, just then, a very different scent.

The scent of battle.

Allies, from all across Avalon, marched swiftly toward him. Muscular centaurs, stamping their hooves, loped to his side. Close behind came men and women who carried rakes and staffs and swords, elves who bore great hunting bows, and dwarves who shouldered double-bladed axes. Plus many other creatures ranging from burly bears to tiny field mice who brought nothing but their brave hearts.

More allies, too, dotted the sky. Eagles swooped down from the heights, hawks with bright red tails glided nearer, and owls floated out of the trees. Soon the air reverberated with their screeches, hoots, and cries.

Yet Basilgarrad peered past them all. For he was watching a dark swarm of jagged-winged warriors that had just appeared over the horizon. Fast they flew, coming closer by the second. He knew them all too well: fire dragons—over a hundred of them.

His nostrils flared. He could smell, even at such a distance, their charred scales and bloodstained claws. And he knew that only he had any hope of stopping them.

The great green dragon shifted his gaze—and what he saw made him dig his claws into the turf. Flamelon warriors! An immense mass of those battle-hardened warriors, trained beneath the smoky volcanoes of Fireroot, started to stream onto the meadow. Armor glinting, they marched steadily nearer. With them came powerful catapults, great machines that could fling heavy stones and vats of boiling oil. They also brought one more contraption, a pyramid-shaped tower so large that it took more than fifty flamelons to drag it across the ground.

Staring at the huge tower, whose wheels creaked noisily, Basilgarrad released a low, wrathful growl. *What in the name of Avalon is that thing?* he asked himself. *Whatever it is, I don't like it. Not at all.*

Although the mysterious tower made him feel uneasy, he quickly forgot about it, for his thoughts had turned to a far greater concern. The fate of his world, the Great Tree whose early days he had witnessed so long ago and whose many wonders he had seen over the centuries. Avalon was, as his friend Merlin once said, more than just a truly remarkable place. It was, in fact, an *idea*—that so many diverse creatures and realms could live together in peace, at least for a time.

That time, he knew, was now dead. But would Avalon itself die, as well? That depended on the outcome of this monumental clash. For this was going to be the first—and, most likely, the last—time all of Avalon's foes and defenders would face each other in battle.

As he scanned the approaching fire dragons and the fearsome battalion of flamelon warriors, he growled deep in his throat. He knew that if he and his loyal allies failed on this day, no one would be left to protect their world. Their homes, their dreams, their families and friends—even his beloved Marnya—would all be lost.

Forever.

His growl swelled into a rumble so loud that several centaurs reared up in surprise, their forelegs kicking at the air. *We must win this battle today!* His huge snout wrinkled. *Not just to defeat this enemy, and not just to save our loved ones. But for another reason, as well.*

"I must survive this day," he vowed, his voice rumbling like thunder. "To find and kill that evil monster behind all this!"

He thumped his tail, shaking with rage and frustration. He didn't know where to find that shadowy beast who had caused this war, promising priceless jewels to the dragons and unrivalled power to the flamelons. All he knew was that its secret lair was somewhere in Avalon—and that it served the wicked warlord of the spirit realm, Rhita Gawr. If only he knew where to look, he could destroy the beast and finally bring this horror to an end. And unless he did that, the threat to Avalon would only grow worse.

Grinding his rows of jagged teeth, he added in a somber tone, "The truth is, even if I do prevail today, there is no way to find that monster. No way at all."

"But there *is*."

Basilgarrad cocked his head and saw, peering up at him, Tressimir, the young historian of the wood elves. "What do you mean?" demanded the dragon. "Speak quickly!"

Tressimir reached into his weathered leather satchel and pulled out a folded piece of parchment. "This is a map. A magical map, from Krystallus. He wanted you to have it—to help you save Avalon."

Basilgarrad watched, glancing anxiously at the approaching enemies, as Tressimir unfolded the parchment. "This map can tell you where to find anything at all. Just concentrate on what you want to find. But first I must warn you."

"About what?"

"This map," declared the elf, "can be used only once. So whatever you want to find, you must be absolutely sure."

"I am sure!"

"Then concentrate your thoughts."

Filling his mind with the shadowy beast, as well as the terrors it had brought to Avalon, Basilgarrad stared at the parchment. Nothing happened. He thought harder, his whole enormous body trembling with exertion. Still nothing.

The parchment remained utterly blank.

Dismayed, he glanced at the swarm of fire dragons advancing across the sky. And at the army of flamelons, dragging their mysterious tower. Then, one last time, he looked at the parchment, silently cursing himself for being foolish enough to let it raise his hopes.

It was changing! The map's edges darkened to a rich golden hue, as tan-colored clouds started to swirl across its face. He spotted, in one corner, a decorative compass, whose arrow suddenly began to spin faster and faster. Meanwhile, the clouds coalesced into shapes. Recognizable shapes.

Avalon! All the root-realms appeared, then six out of seven vanished as the map focused on just one—Mudroot. Veering northward, the image moved all the way to the farthest reaches of the realm, revealing the dark, shifting outlines of a swamp. And deep within that swamp . . . an eerie red glow.

"The Haunted Marsh!" exclaimed Tressimir.

"So that's where you are hiding," growled the dragon through clenched teeth. "I will find you. Oh, yes, I will find you."

He rustled his gargantuan wings. "First, though, I have a battle to fight."

Just as Basilgarrad started to open his wings, Tressimir cried out in surprise. The map began to smoke, sizzling between his fingers. He dropped it, and at that instant, it burst into flames. Seconds later, nothing remained but ashes—and one tiny scrap that drifted slowly to the ground.

Deftly, Basilgarrad clasped the ragged bit of paper between the tips of two claws. The scrap, still smoking, looked more like a flake of charcoal than anything valuable. Let alone magical. Only a barely noticeable mark on its unburned edge, the golden arrow from the decorative compass, gave any hint of its remarkable origin.

On an impulse, he tucked the smoldering scrap into the gap above an iridescent green scale on his shoulder. Why, he couldn't explain. He only knew that he didn't want to part with it. At least not yet.

Then, opening his wide wings, he released a thunderous roar that filled the sky. All who heard it knew, beyond doubt, that the great battle for Avalon had begun.

1: THE ONSLAUGHT

Hope is sometimes fleeting, but always precious. Sad to say, when that battle began, most of my companions had no hope at all.

With a mighty roar that shook trees many leagues away, the most powerful dragon in the history of Avalon leaped into the sky.

But even as his enormous green wings opened wide and started to beat, slapping the air forcefully as they carried him higher, Basilgarrad glanced down at the spot where the ashes from the magical map were still drifting down to the grass. Silently, he repeated his vow: *I will find you. Whatever it takes, I will go to the Haunted Marsh—and find you.*

"But first," he said aloud, peering at the army of fire dragons flying swiftly toward him, "I have a small task to perform."

Eyes alight, he roared once again—the roar of a dragon plunging into battle.

Above him, a canyon eagle screeched, calling all the assembled hawks, owls, and eagles to their leader's side. As Basilgarrad rose higher to join them, his huge dragon wings shadowed the ground below—rolling grasslands that, in peaceful times, held only wildflower meadows and the bubbling springs that fed Woodroot's fabled River Relentless. For ages this place had been one of the most serene in Avalon. All that would soon change.

For now those meadows held a swollen tide of flamelon warriors, so seasoned that they marched in absolute unison, as if the metal of their armor and swords had been melted down and forged into a single weapon of death. From this altitude, he could see their many catapults, along with some smoking contraptions that he guessed were flamethrowers. And he could see, once again, the huge, pyramid-shaped tower whose ominous purpose could only be guessed.

Ogre's eyeballs! he cursed to himself. *What could that tower be?*

His gaze shifted from the flamelons and their machinery to his own scattered allies. Centaurs stamped their sturdy hooves, great bears roared angrily, elves readied their bows and arrows, while a few dozen brave men, women, and dwarves wielded spears and battle-axes. But seeing his supporters didn't fill him with hope. Rather, he shuddered at this aerial view. For it revealed just how vastly outnumbered his supporters were—and how they lacked the training, experience, and sophisticated weaponry of their foes. They looked less like an army, Avalon's last line of defense, than like a group of tattered moths about to be consumed by a blast of flames.

All they have, thought Basilgarrad grimly, *is their love for this world*. He flapped his wide wings, lifting his mountainous bulk so high that his massive tail stretched out fully behind him. *Well, I suppose they do have one more thing on their side.*

He suddenly curled his tail and snapped it, whiplike, against the air. The explosion smote the sky, louder than a hundred claps of thunder. Several of the approaching fire dragons faltered, veered out of formation, and probably would have turned tail and fled if their commanders hadn't roared angrily at them.

Allowing himself a smirk, Basilgarrad finished his thought. *They still have me.*

At that instant, twenty fire dragons at the attackers' leading edge simultaneously released a superheated blast of flames. Fire poured over Basilgarrad, so intense that he turned his face away to protect his eyes. Hot flames slammed into the protective scales of his neck and chest, blackening their once-radiant surfaces, but leaving him unharmed.

The brave birds flying at his side didn't fare so well. Two red-tailed hawks and one peregrine falcon with silver-tipped wings burst into flames, shrieked in agony, and plunged to their deaths. The canyon eagle's tail feathers caught on fire, though a swift tap from Basilgarrad's wing tip extinguished that. Meanwhile, far below, the shower of sparks fell onto the allied forces, causing screams from several whose hair, clothes, or skin had been burned.

Basilgarrad roared with rage—a powerful blast of air that blew backward several attackers' wings. Yet his roar, alas, carried no flames. As a woodland dragon, he couldn't breathe fire, no matter how hard he tried. No amount of volume could change that fact; as loud as his roar was, it seemed a weak response.

A raucous, rasping laughter echoed across the sky. "Is that all you can do?" taunted the fire dragons' leader. "That pitiable little snarl?"

He laughed again, a sound that scorched almost as badly as flames. A huge scarlet dragon, he was half again as large as his heftiest soldiers—though still smaller than Basilgarrad. His eyes blazed wrathfully, and his wings slapped the air with a vengeance. Upon his chin lay the stubbly remains of a once-prominent beard. It had been forcibly removed, long ago, by the only dragon who had ever dared to face him in battle: Basilgarrad himself.

"Well, well," answered the great green dragon, his own eyes glowing bright. He beat his wings slowly, hovering in place. "If it isn't Lo Valdearg, that orange snake with wings. I thought you wouldn't dare attack me again—at least until you grew another beard."

The fire dragon roared angrily, shooting a spray of sparks from his nostrils. "I do dare!" he bellowed, as sparks rained down on his snout.

"Only when you are flanked by a hundred soldiers," retorted Basilgarrad. His eyebrows, studded with iridescent scales, arched. "Because you wouldn't have the courage to attack me by yourself. No, without your army to help, you are afraid to fight."

"I would fight," boomed Lo Valdearg. "And I shall."

"Not likely! You are as cowardly as ever."

The fire dragon snorted with rage. "I am no coward!"

Basilgarrad's brows lifted higher. Would his foe really take the bait? Whatever his chances might be against this whole army—and they were slim at best—they would improve dramatically if he could tempt the leader to fight one-on-one.

Lo Valdearg spun in the air. "Wait here!" he commanded his soldiers. At once, the fire dragons ceased their advance. They hovered in the sky, flanking their leader as he flew alone into combat.

Unable to keep himself from grinning, Basilgarrad glided nearer, watching Lo Valdearg warily. At the same time, the fire dragon approached, raking the air viciously with his claws.

"Now we shall see who is truly the greatest dragon," rumbled Lo Valdearg as he started to circle his opponent.

"Yes, we shall." Basilgarrad, too, began to circle. "And we shall also see who is the greatest fool."

"That," snarled Lo Valdearg, "would be you." He grinned wickedly, showing hundreds of murderous teeth. "For only a complete fool would turn his back on his enemy!"

Too late, Basilgarrad realized the trap. While Lo Valdearg had always been ready to fight, he'd never intended to keep his word and fight alone. Instead, by circling, he had cleverly maneuvered Basilgarrad into position to be attacked from behind by an entire army of dragons.

The sky exploded with a terrible onslaught of flames—all directed at Basilgarrad. Amidst that deadly inferno of fire and smoke, he couldn't even be seen. The mighty roars of dragons, the sizzling crackle of flames, and the surprised screeches of hawks and eagles all filled the air. And with them came another sound—one dragon's raucous, rasping laughter.

The battle for Avalon had ended, it seemed, before it had even begun.

2: INFERNO

Dying gets easier with a little practice.

For a long, agonizing moment, Basilgarrad's supporters on the ground stared up at the sky. Thick black clouds billowed, surrounding the crackling inferno of superheated flames. Somewhere inside all that smoke and fire was the great green dragon—or whatever remained of him.

Centaurs, whinnying anxiously, paced on the turf; elves and humans stood transfixed, mouths agape; dwarves dropped their axes in horror. Even the flamelon warriors, sensing impending victory, halted their advance to watch.

A shower of sparks fell to the ground, striking many onlookers. Still they did not take their eyes off the sky. As the clouds slowly started to thin, the intense blaze diminished. Figures became visible—dozens of hovering fire dragons, whose jagged wings seemed to fan the remaining flames. One fire dragon in particular, an orange behemoth much larger than the rest, flew in triumphant circles, waiting to deliver the final blow.

A shape suddenly burst out of the center of the flames—an immensely long and powerful tail that belonged to a dragon.

So crusted with charcoal that it seemed more black than green, the tail whipped out of the blaze with lightning speed. Its massive club slammed full force into the orange dragon's chest.

Lo Valdearg bellowed in pain as he bowled over backward, flipped upside down by the surprise blow. Before the fire dragon could right himself, Basilgarrad emerged from the inferno. He roared as he attacked, his green eyes aglow, his powerful wings slapping the air, his enormous tail already curled to strike again. The heralded defender of Avalon, called Wings of Peace by many throughout the realms, was very much alive.

And very much enraged.

A loud cheer erupted from his allies on the grasslands below. Instantly, the ground clash resumed. Though the green dragon's supporters were greatly outnumbered, and though the flamelons pelted them mercilessly with stones from catapults and burning bundles of oil-soaked wood from flame hurlers, they fought with renewed strength. And renewed hope. Basilgarrad had survived!

Centaurs charged boldly into the middle of the flamelons' battalion, galloping full speed, kicking their hooves to drive a wedge between the warriors. Bears lumbered right behind, slamming their paws into the flamelons with such force that their armored chest plates crushed and broke apart. And many flamelon bones and skulls shared the same fate. Dwarves, small but sturdy, swung their axes, while men and women slashed with broadswords and spears. At the same time, elven archers loosed volley after volley of well-aimed arrows, dropping so many attackers that the flamelons' bodies piled high, forming bloody ridges across the ground.

Yet even such ferocity could not stop the flamelons' advance. With terrible efficiency, they overwhelmed the defenders, slashing and pummeling anyone who dared stand in their way. The brave allies, already few in number, grew steadily fewer. Many of them, even in the throes of death, looked again to the sky, hoping that Basilgarrad would prevail against the fire dragons—and return to the ground in time to save at least some of their lives.

The instant he burst out of the inferno, roaring wrathfully, Basilgarrad swooped down on Lo Valdearg. Still struggling to right himself from the blow to his chest, the fire dragons' leader feared for his life. Fortunately, he didn't have any such concern for the lives of his soldiers; they were merely his shield. He shrieked for help—so loudly he popped several scales off his throat.

More than thirty fire dragons heeded his cry. They hurled themselves directly at this enormous dragon, swarming over him like a mass of leather-winged bees. Despite their vastly superior numbers, and their outrage at this traitor to their kind who had dared to strike their leader, they found themselves facing something quite unexpected—a foe of unimaginable strength whose outrage exceeded their own.

Basilgarrad moved so fast his gigantic body became a blur. His tail smashed into three dragons' heads in rapid succession, tore through several others' wings, then slammed into another one's chest so hard that the beast flew straight into another pair and knocked them out of the sky. All that happened in the first two seconds. Then Basilgarrad got busy.

Spinning like a deadly cyclone, he whirled through the attackers. The bony tips of his wings jabbed at foes' heads, cracking skulls as easily as nutshells, while the wide wings themselves smashed several dragons together and dumped them out in an unconscious heap. His claws, meanwhile, tore at limbs, ripped apart scales, and severed unfortunate heads from their shoulders. Yet nothing caused so much damage as his terrible tail. Swinging and slamming like an unstoppable club, the tail felled dozens of dragons, hurling their limp bodies into the distant sea beyond the borders of the realm.

Even so, Basilgarrad had only begun to warm to his task. His primary goal—to destroy Lo Valdearg once and for all—still eluded him. Every time he caught sight of the treacherous dragon, another host of soldiers attacked, giving Lo Valdearg time to escape. Despite the fury of battle, Basilgarrad's sharp eyes continued to scan the skies for his enemy. For he knew that this battle on high would not end until one of them died. And he also knew that Lo Valdearg, like himself, was searching for that very opportunity.

Spying one unusually burly fire dragon, Basilgarrad changed tactics. Pivoting in the air, he wrapped his tail around the soldier's neck, then worked his wings hard to spin himself—and the soldier—in a series of tight circles. The helpless soldier, now a weapon, slammed into dragon after dragon. Wing bones shattered, skulls crunched, and backbones snapped with the impact. Again and again and again.

At last, having cleared the sky of most enemies, Basilgarrad stopped spinning. Only a few fire dragons remained nearby, watching him warily. But Lo Valdearg was not among them.

"Where is that coward?" he growled angrily. "Where did he go?"

Impatiently, he flung aside the battered soldier, tossing him into the trees that bordered the meadow. To his dismay, he spied several dark columns of smoke and spurting flames rising from the forest beyond. *Woodroot—on fire!*

Peering at the smoky columns, he shuddered at the sound that now reached him—hundreds of wailing, shrieking voices crying desperately for help. Birds in their nests, squirrels caught on branches, foxes and badgers choking in their dens, panicked deer dashing for an open clearing. All those lives, as well as those of the trees in this magical forest, would soon end in flames.

Suddenly he caught sight of an orange wing amidst the black smoke. Lo Valdearg! Then he saw the orange dragon breathe a new blast of flames, instantly igniting a grove of ancient cedars. *So this is how he fights! Too scared to face me, he attacks those innocent creatures instead.* Basilgarrad grimaced, creasing his scaly snout, for he now guessed his enemy's true motive: to distract him from demolishing the fire dragons, drawing him into a new fight to save the forest. Meanwhile, Lo Valdearg would continue to evade him, and the flamelons would continue hammering at his allies on the ground.

Those allies, Basilgarrad saw with a quick glance at the battlefield below, were faring badly. Very badly. Bodies of centaurs, elves, men, and women lay everywhere. Though many had died atop a pile of flamelons they had slain, they would fight no longer. And the defenders' numbers were fast dwindling. Even now, several were fighting for their lives against an onslaught of invaders, while catapulted stones smashed all around them.

Wait! Is that . . .

He caught his breath, recognizing one lone dwarf bravely swinging her battle-ax. She stood on top of a fallen fire dragon, charging up and down the lifeless beast's chest to fight off attackers. Her ax whistled as she swung it savagely, knocking back even the most aggressive flamelons. Yet she couldn't hold them at bay much longer.

Though she had grown into an adult, her fierce determination to survive—as well as her father's oversized battle-ax, still taller than she was—reminded Basilgarrad of the young girl whose life he had saved years before. Strings of quartz crystals adorned her curly red hair, clattering whenever she turned her head, the headdress of a leader of the dwarves. That was no surprise, given the fact she came from impressive stock—including her grandmother, Urnalda, whose friendship with a young wizard named Merlin had long inspired bards, and whose name she now bore.

Fierce as she was, though, this youthful Urnalda looked increasingly fatigued. Her ax seemed heavier by the minute; her swings grew steadily more erratic. Meanwhile the flamelons pressed her from all sides, forcing her to swing more wildly.

Beating his wide wings to hold himself aloft, Basilgarrad turned his head back to the forest. Flames were spreading rapidly, consuming elegant spruces and gnarled firs, devouring ancient oaks and young elms along with all the creatures they held. Even a grove of harmona trees, whose branches made wondrous music with every breath of wind, burned uncontrollably. They now shrieked with piercing, atonal screams that scraped like claws against the soul.

The green dragon winced. He knew that this fire would spread across the forest until it destroyed most, if not all, of Woodroot. His home realm. But how could he stop it? After all, he didn't possess any magic that could stop a fire. He couldn't exhale a fountain of water to douse the flames, nor use his ability to cast smells to help. And even if he did have some useful magic, he didn't have much time.

What to do? he agonized. For the very first time since this battle began, he felt torn by indecision. If he hesitated to join the battle, Urnalda—and many other loyal defenders of Avalon—would surely die. And if he didn't somehow stop those flames . . . his treasured forest, his longtime home, would perish.

If only he had more help! It always seemed to come down to him, and him alone, to save the day for Avalon. Even Merlin, the most powerful person ever to call this world home, whose magical seed gave birth to the Great Tree itself, had abandoned Basilgarrad, leaving him to defend Avalon alone.

Why did Merlin leave? To help a young king, he had claimed, on the faraway world called Earth. But the dragon—

Basil, as the wizard called him—always suspected other reasons. Personal ones. Selfish ones. In simple truth, the wizard had departed to nurse his grief over the death of his beloved wife, Hallia—and the painful estrangement of his son, Krystallus.

Not reason enough, grumbled the dragon. He snorted angrily. And where, for that matter, were Avalon's other great warriors when he needed them? None of the surviving giants had come to this battle, though they'd fought bravely in the past. Not even his old friend Shim had come to help. Some said that the giant had gone into hiding ever since the terrible combat of the Withered Spring, but no one knew why. What could be his reasons? Selfish ones, most likely.

Even Rhia, such a powerful force for peace in years past, had abandoned him. Just as she had abandoned Avalon in its time of need!

Basilgarrad slashed his tail through the air and bellowed with frustration. Were none of his friends truly that? Were none of them more reliable than Aylah, the wind sister who blew through many places but never stayed anywhere for long—not even for a friend?

"Once again," he grumbled, "it's all up to me." He ground his spear-sharp teeth, squeezing his jaws so tight that no gap remained—except the one space where he'd lost a tooth long ago. "But what should I do?"

His enormous eyes, sparkling with the magic of élano, flicked back and forth. Save the forest? Or his allies? He had precious little time left to do much for either. Whatever he chose, it must be *now*.

The idea came in a flash. Without pausing to take another look at the battlefield, or even to think the idea through, he slapped his wings against the air. Swiftly, he flew toward the blazing forest.

Veering in the air above the conflagration, Basilgarrad spread his great wings to their widest. Like a titanic hand from the sky, he fell straight on top of the fire, smothering the burning trees. A loud *whhhoooooomph!* filled the air, replacing the incessant crackle of flames and explosions of sap.

He sat still for several seconds, grinding the smoldering trees under his broad wings. Smoke curled up from the edges, but this was the final, ashen smoke of a fire extinguished. At the edge of one wing, he spied a lone spurt of flame in a lilac bush beyond his reach. One quick whip of his tail, crushing the fire under its massive weight, took care of that.

Raising his head, he scanned the skies. No stray columns of smoke remained—and no sign of Lo Valdearg. *I will find you, cowardly scum! And when I do . . .*

He didn't finish the thought. For his mind had already turned to the murderous flamelon warriors and what awaited them. Rubbing his wings into the charred forest beneath him one last time, he leaped into the air, spun a wide turn, and flew back into battle.

3: BIGNESS

Perspectives can always change, but never more than when you go from outside to inside.

Three flamelon warriors climbed the fallen fire dragon where Urnalda still battled, attacking her from different sides. Simultaneously, they charged at her, their armored boots scraping on the scarlet scales of the dragon's chest.

Their grim faces and copper-colored eyes betrayed no emotion as they stabbed at her with double-edged swords, forged for extra strength in the molten River of Fire. Working with practiced coordination, they timed their blows so that she couldn't pause for even an instant. Blades slashed incessantly at her face, arms, and legs—which, though short, wore no protective armor.

The dwarf maiden fought back fiercely, swinging her battle-ax with added zeal. But she panted hoarsely, grunting with effort each time she swung the heavy weapon. One of the flamelons slashed at her knee, slicing the skin and drawing blood. Another drew her off balance with a false thrust at her face, then lunged hard at her chest. Just barely, she knocked his sword aside with the ax handle. But the blow nudged her backward a step too far, making her boot slide off the dragon's chest.

Urnalda wobbled, standing on one leg. Desperately, she leaned into her attackers, struggling to keep herself from pitching over backward. She managed to swing her ax again, connecting with a warrior's temple. His helmet split instantly. With a moan, he tumbled off the dragon.

But his companions, sensing their opportunity, lunged at her with all their strength. One of their blades whizzed past her neck, so close that it sliced off a lock of red hair and the pair of quartz crystals tied to it. They clattered on the scarlet scales by her boot.

Precarious though her stance was, she tried to swing the ax again. But its weight threw her completely off balance. She took one hand off the handle, clawing at the air, trying to keep from falling.

Meanwhile, a warrior's sword tip slashed at her face. The blade grazed her chin. Instinctively, she leaned back—

Too far! She fell over backward, straight at the flamelon warriors who had gathered below. They cheered as they raised their swords, savoring this chance to end her life.

A gigantic claw hooked the strap of her breastplate, catching her before she reached them. A gargantuan shadow fell over the warriors, turning their cheers into gasps of astonishment. That was the last sound they made before Basilgarrad's clubbed tail smashed down on top of them.

As she rose into the sky, carried by the enormous dragon, Urnalda gazed up at her savior. Clutching her battle-ax, she peered into one of his glowing green eyes. Then she cocked her head, clinking the quartz crystals strung through her hair.

"Bad timing," she said gruffly, turning her mouth down in a scowl. "I was just about to slay them all!"

Basilgarrad's eye kept watching her. He didn't speak, but merely flapped his immense wings, lifting them higher.

Slowly, her scowl melted into a grin. "But I thank you anyway."

"You've grown a bit since I saw you last."

"You haven't," she replied. "Though you didn't really need to."

Basilgarrad chuckled, a rumble from deep in his throat. "Try to keep yourself alive now, will you?"

"Absolutely." She twirled the ax in her hands. "I have some more work to do."

"As do I," thundered the dragon.

Urnalda scowled again. "Basilgarrad," she said, her voice suddenly sounding worried, "beware of that evil-looking tower, will you? The one shaped like a pyramid. Never have I seen it before in battle. And I fear it is meant for . . ."

"What?"

"For *you*." The dwarf's eyes shone like fire coals. "For harming—even destroying—you."

Despite his own concerns about the tower, Basilgarrad merely snorted.

Her scowl deepened, filling her face with lines. "We need you to survive, great friend. For Avalon."

Now it was the dragon's turn to frown. "To finally save Avalon, there is one last battle I will need to fight. In the Haunted Marsh."

She shook her head, clattering her crystals. "The Marsh? What could be there but rot and poison and certain death?"

"Someone I must destroy," he answered with a snarl.

Urnalda peered at him for a few seconds, as his wings continued to pump, carrying her to another part of the battle-field. "You dragons," she said at last, "do strange business."

"Stranger than you know," replied Basilgarrad.

He tilted his wings, gliding slightly to the left. With one claw, he pointed at a grassy hill. "How does that spot look to you?"

Both of them gazed at the hill. Only yesterday, a pure spring had flowed from its slope, cascading down to the meadow below, carelessly splashing on rocks and spraying bluebell flowers. Today, though, the rise was smeared with mud, blood, and the wreckage of a toppled catapult. Atop the hill stood a bedraggled band of elves. Though expert archers, they were weak and wounded—and down to their very last arrows. One of them, Basilgarrad noticed, was Tressimir, who had shown him the magical map just before the battle began.

"That spot will do fine," answered the dwarf. Grimly, she eyed the flamelon warriors who had gathered at the base of the hill. Smelling a slaughter, they pressed toward the struggling elves, marching higher as the arrows grew scarcer.

The dragon swooped down. Tressimir, the first elf to see him, shouted with jubilation. Before most of the other elves knew what was happening, Basilgarrad landed with a tremendous thud beside the hill, skidding across the grass and crushing more than fifty flamelons.

Several surviving warriors scurried away, tripping over themselves to escape this gargantuan beast from the sky. Urnalda, meanwhile, hopped down to the ground. She started to chase after them, waving her battle-ax, then stopped and turned back to the dragon who had saved her life. For an instant their gazes met. She nodded, then spun around and raced after the flamelons.

"Now," declared the dragon, "back to work."

He leaped into the air, just as a vat of boiling oil exploded on the ground. The scalding hot liquid sprayed everywhere, hitting several of the elves. A few drops spattered Basilgarrad's eye. He roared in sudden pain and blinked away the oil. Then, as his vision cleared, he focused his gaze on the catapult that had hurled the vat.

Two wingbeats later, he plunged from the sky above the catapult. Swinging his tail like a massive hammer, he smashed the structure into countless pieces. Wood chips, cables, and the unlucky flamelons who had been on top of the frame flew in all directions.

Satisfied that the catapult would do no more damage, he

flew off again. Just then he spotted, not far away, the evil tower. Scores of flamelons were working hard, moving the giant structure into place at the middle of the battlefield.

Still other warriors climbed onto the three massive ridge-poles of the triangular frame that rose to a point high above the ground. Each of those ridgepoles had been made from dozens of ironwood trees joined end to end—trees whose reddish-brown trunks, both sturdy and straight, gleamed with a metallic sheen. At the very top, the ridgepoles had been spliced into a perfect point and wrapped with iron cable for maximum strength. The whole structure looked like the skele-ton of a huge pyramid.

Coasting for a wingbeat, the dragon scrutinized the tower, watching the soldiers string webs of wires along the frame. Those wires attached to hundreds of spiky levers that ran the full length of the ridgepoles, forming a complex rigging. Far below, more soldiers worked on the huge wooden crate at the base, hammering planks, tying ropes, and affixing more wires to its edges.

Basilgarrad's ears swiveled doubtfully. What could that tower be? And what did its crate contain? His huge wings beat the air as he swept toward the mysterious structure.

Suddenly he caught sight of a small creature at the edge of the battlefield. Though he couldn't tell what sort of being it was, its plight was unmistakable—and dire. Trapped in the highest branches of an old, gnarled oak tree, it was being pelted by stones and spears hurled by more than twenty flamelons gathered around the trunk. From their raucous laughter and boisterous antics, it was clear that they weren't so much attacking the little creature as bullying it. They wouldn't stop until it fell to the ground where they could stomp and stab it to death.

I hate bullies! he thought. *Always have.* Shifting direction, he pumped his wings to race to the creature's rescue.

As he flapped those huge wings—so big they could embrace an entire lake—he grinned, recalling that he'd once been as small as that little animal. Or even smaller. *But no more!* He certainly wasn't small now. And he would never be small again!

Nearing the tree, he raised his head in surprise. *Wait! Do I know that little fellow?*

His wingbeats slowed as he peered more closely. Sure enough, it was an immature dragon, whose bony wings looked as thin as paper, and whose scarlet and purple scales were as tiny as acorns. *Why, yes. That's Ganta, the spunky young rascal!*

Basilgarrad blinked his wide eyes. He couldn't possibly forget his own nephew, who was always eager—too eager—to fight. Or their first meeting, when Basilgarrad was still small, which had nearly turned into a battle to the death. Now here he was, in the midst of the fight for Avalon, a fight that had set both land and sky aflame.

Just as he reached the oak tree, the green dragon spun a sharp turn. He dipped one wing so low it scraped against the ground, scooping up turf, swords, helmets, a few dead birds—and almost all the flamelons under the tree. The few who escaped capture sprinted away as fast as they could. Their companions, meanwhile, rolled into a heap in the cupped wing, unable to do more than shriek in terror.

Basilgarrad didn't have time to listen. Raising his wing, he flung those flamelons across the forest, all the way to the horizon and beyond. Wherever they landed, it must have been brutally painful. The dragon watched their flailing bodies vanish from sight, then nodded in satisfaction.

He veered lower and landed thunderously, bowling over some nearby trees and sending tremors across the battlefield. Slowly, he stretched his head toward the tree, meeting the incredulous gaze of Ganta. The young dragon, no bigger than one of Basilgarrad's scales, could only stare with his orange-hued eyes.

"Hello, Ganta."

"Er . . . hello, master Basil." Nervously, the youngster rubbed his snout with his little wing.

Noting the slender scar on the tip of Ganta's nose, a souvenir from their first meeting, Basilgarrad resisted a grin and spoke firmly. "This is a dangerous place to be. Where is your mother?"

Scampering a bit farther out on his branch, the young dragon answered, "She's back at the lair in Stoneroot with my brothers and sisters. But I"—he swallowed, causing a ripple to roll down his thin neck—"I wanted to fight. For Avalon."

"Really? You didn't just want to join a big battle, whatever it was about?"

Ganta shook his wings indignantly. "No, master Basil. Truly! I do like a fight, it's true. But this time . . . it's, well . . . a chance to be *big*."

His uncle's gigantic eyebrow lifted. "Big?"

"Don't you remember?" piped Ganta eagerly. "That day we met in the dragongrass by the geyser? You said something I'd never heard before, something I needed time to understand. You said . . . being big isn't about what you weigh— but about what you *do*."

Basilgarrad couldn't suppress a grin any longer. *Maybe there's hope for this young troublemaker after all.* His voice, however, remained stern. "You've got to go home, Ganta. It's dangerous here. Too dangerous for a youngster who is barely old enough to fly."

"But I *can* fly, master Basil! I can fly almost as fast as my mother. And someday I'll be able to breathe fire, too, just like her!"

The great head shook from side to side. "Go now, Ganta. When you can finally breathe fire, then at least you'll be able to defend yourself. That's when you can join this kind of fight."

"That could be years and years!" he squealed. "This battle will probably be over by then."

"I certainly hope so," declared Basilgarrad. "And now"—he backed his massive body away from the tree, preparing to leap skyward—"I must get back to work."

The greatest dragon in Avalon stretched his wings and gave a mighty flap, causing a rush of wind that shook every branch of the oak tree. As he rose into the sky, Ganta watched in awe. The little fellow held tight to his swaying branch, refusing to blink so he wouldn't miss even a single stroke of those mighty wings. They belonged, after all, to the biggest creature he'd ever seen.

4: A New Gleam

Vision, even for a dragon, is woefully unreliable. What you see with great clarity may not be real; what you cannot see may be the ultimate reality.

Soaring over the battlefield, Basilgarrad seemed everywhere at once. His wing tip smashed another catapult, sending up an explosion of splinters. Then, for good measure, his claws scooped up the catapult's supply of boulders (along with a few unwary soldiers) and dropped them on top of a column of flamelons. He plucked a young priest out of danger, only an instant before a poison-tipped spear flew through the same spot—then circled back to save the feisty squirrel who normally rode in the priest's tunic pocket, but who had fallen out during the rescue. He slammed his tail into groups of flamelons, scattering soldiers and weapons across the grass.

Just one swipe of that tail was all it took to destroy a pair of flamethrowers, whose metal frames buckled on impact and whose fiery cauldrons exploded into shards. The soldiers who operated them fared no better. And it took only one heavy stamp of his foot to grind all their burning bales of oil-soaked hay (plus a few more soldiers) into the ground.

Today, thought Basilgarrad grimly, *I don't really deserve the name Wings of Peace.*

Some of the defenders whose lives he saved were so exhausted from battle that they fell limp to the ground the instant he set them down. Others reacted somewhat differently. As soon as he put down the haggard old warrior Babd Catha—whose full name, earned over years of hunting murderous ogres, was Babd Catha, the Ogres' Bane—she started cursing him fiercely for interrupting her sword fight with six flamelon soldiers. It was as if he'd stopped her from chowing down a slice of strawberry pie, or silenced her in the middle of singing a cherished tune. Just to make sure he fully understood her outrage, she concluded her curses by swatting his gigantic chin with her sword.

"Never do that again, ye scaly upstart!" she admonished, her brown eyes ablaze. "Now I need to go find all six of them pests an' finish the job!"

The dragon, who had heard many stories about this old warrior, grinned at her fighting spirit. He couldn't even begin to guess her age, although he knew that she'd lived a very long time, possibly due to a few drops of wizard's blood that Merlin once gave her to heal her wounds. Legends told that she had been one of the first people to help Elen, Merlin's mother, found the new order of Avalon. And that she had started her battles against ogres when only a child, after a marauding band killed both her parents.

He remembered something else. Some bards claimed that since that brutal attack on her family occurred in a snowstorm, the only thing in the world that Babd Catha actually feared was snow. A few went even further and said that the touch of a single snowflake would force her to retreat. Basilgarrad seriously doubted the truth of those stories, especially now that he'd seen all the scars on her face and arms from a lifetime of battles. Tempted as he was to ask her how she really felt about snow, he knew this was not the best time.

Instead, he bowed his huge ears and said, "My apologies, great warrior."

Such humble words are most unusual from a dragon, but Babd Catha didn't show any trace of surprise. After all, to her mind, an apology was certainly due. She merely grumbled, "All right, dragon. Jest don't interrupt me again."

With that, the feisty old warrior spun around, raised her broadsword, and plunged back into the fray.

As he watched Babd Catha charge back into battle, Basilgarrad turned his head toward the dark tower in the center of the fighting—the only flamelon contraption he hadn't yet destroyed. Was it perhaps some sort of catapult? That might explain the web of wires and levers along its pyramidal frame. Yet would a catapult so huge actually work? And what would it throw? The structure didn't seem to hold any stones, oil vats, or other dangerous objects. In fact, it held nothing but that massive wooden crate at its base.

Truth was, the structure didn't look dangerous. Nothing about its actual appearance gave any genuine cause for alarm. It merely *smelled* somehow dangerous.

Peering at it from across the battlefield, he shifted his bulk on the muddy ground. Then he noticed something strange. All the flamelon soldiers he'd seen crawling over the tower, working on its various components, had vanished. Now not a single warrior could be found anywhere on its frame, wires, or base. Even the soldiers fighting near the tower's base seemed to keep their distance—ignoring it, as if the whole contraption was not there.

That's curious, he thought, scrunching his massive nose in puzzlement.

Glancing at the sky above, he searched again for Lo Valdearg, the only target even more tempting than the strange tower. Seeing no sign of the fire dragon, not even a stray trail of black smoke, he growled furiously and thumped his gargantuan tail on the ground. *Time to destroy that tower!* He rustled his great wings, preparing to fly. *The flamelons' weapons have killed too many people already.*

His own words prompted him to scan the battlefield one more time—more closely than he'd done before. Everywhere, amidst the frenzied battle, he saw the corpses of his allies, more than he wanted to count. Fallen eagles and owls, trampled by flamelons' boots, peppered the ground. Brawny bears, once so powerful, lay forever still. Men and women, elves and dwarves, and more than a few sturdy centaurs, were now mud-splattered bodies left to rot.

The memory of a dark, writhing monster filled his mind, obscuring the carnage at least for a moment. The monster whose wicked schemes had spawned this war. The monster whose lair was deep in the Haunted Marsh.

When this battle is over, he thought with a savage snarl, *I will hunt you down! And end your horrors once and for all.*

Yet . . . would even that vengeance, that triumph, outweigh all these losses? All these needless, innocent deaths? Basilgarrad surveyed the corpses, bloody and maimed, that surrounded him. There were so many people—good people—who, despite all his efforts, he hadn't been able to save!

He ground his jaws together, scraping his titanic teeth. Had those fallen warriors died in vain? What could possibly justify so many deaths?

"Nothing," he grumbled aloud, his voice as bitter as his mood. "They were fools—just like me. And I've been the worst fool of all. Thinking all this time I was fighting for something more than myself—for my friends, my world."

He snorted. "Well, most of my friends—Merlin, Rhia, Aylah—have left. And my world, what's left of it, reeks of death. The truth is, I'm *alone* in this. Fighting for what I want: revenge, and a life of my own."

Basilgarrad tensed his legs, ready to leap skyward as he'd done so many times before. There was, however, a new gleam in his eye. He would keep fighting this battle to the end; he would still hunt down Lo Valdearg and that monster in the Haunted Marsh. Yet now he would do those things not for some high ideal—but for sweet revenge. To repay those terrible foes for all the suffering, agony, and death they'd caused.

He nodded grimly. *I'll smash them all! Then, when I'm through, I'll finally do something I've been meaning to do for a*

*very long time. I'll go find Marnya . . . and see what kind of
future we might have.*

The memory of the water dragon's azure blue eyes—and
her eagerness to be the first of her kind ever to fly—made his
heart pound within his vast chest. Would Marnya feel the same
way? Would she want to be with such a fool as him? It was
time to find out. Yes, and high time he started thinking about
what was best for his own life!

He focused his gaze on the strange, unmanned tower.
He'd quickly destroy it—and then do the same to the rest of
his enemies. Because, out of sheer anger and vengeance, that
was what he wanted to do.

Basilgarrad leaped into the sky, flapped his wide wings,
and flew toward the tower.

5: THE TOWER

Ah, life's little surprises! They can make any day unforgettable . . . or make it your last.

"One flick of my tail should do it," said Basilgarrad confidently as he neared the flamelons' mysterious tower. Wind whistled past his ears, vibrating the countless green hairs that grew within them.

He gave his wings another powerful flap. Where, he wondered, would be the best place to strike? At the top of the pyramidal frame, where so many wires were attached? Or down lower, at the immense crate that seemed to be the tower's foundation?

At the top, he decided. *Right at the point. That will smash the whole thing to splinters.*

Yet even as he made his decision, unanswered questions bubbled in the cauldron of his mind. Why, unlike the rest of the flamelons' towers, were no soldiers anywhere on this contraption? And why, in all this fighting, hadn't it been used? *Especially now*, he puzzled, *when the flamelons need every weapon they have?*

Circling the tower, he pushed aside any lingering doubts.

It's just a structure, after all. Made from wood and wire and rope—nothing I can't easily demolish.

Veering upward, he slapped the air with his wings to lift himself to a vertical position so that he could give maximum power to his tail. Meanwhile, he curled the massive tail upward, arching his back. At precisely the right moment, he did what he'd done hundreds of times before: He slammed the heavy club down on his target.

Instantly, the tower exploded—but not in the way he'd expected. Instead of splintering on impact, the wooden beams of the frame buckled inward and slid sideways on rollers, releasing the myriad of levers. All those levers flipped, engaging rows of gears that had lain hidden in grooves beneath the beams. As the gears started to turn in synchronized rotations, wires all over the tower tightened, creaking with tension.

Ropes burst apart, freeing the doors that covered the massive crate at the base. Unseen springs released, throwing open the doors. With a loud *whooooosh,* a gigantic net shot out of the crate, flying straight up into the sky—

And into Basilgarrad.

Before he realized what had happened, the dragon was completely ensnared. Thick, strong netting wrapped around his wings, his legs, his jaws, and even his mighty tail. He fought, still airborne, to free himself, but every move tightened the grip of the net. His wings, pinned to his sides, couldn't break the strands, no matter how vigorously he tried. Even his jaws, with all their perilous teeth, couldn't open a crack.

Suddenly helpless, Basilgarrad started to fall. Time seemed to slow down as he spun through the air, yet what he wanted was to stop time altogether. He roared through his closed jaws—a roar unlike any he'd ever made. For mixed with all the rage and surprise came an unmistakable hint of terror.

Trapped! I'm trapped! his mind screamed as he struggled to break free.

His gargantuan body crashed to the ground, shattering the remains of the tower. Shards of wood, lines of wire, levers, and gears flew in every direction. But it made no difference. The tower, specially designed to ensnare Basilgarrad, had done its work.

The moment he crashed, the battlefield abruptly fell silent. Sword fights ceased, soldiers froze, skirmishes ended. It was as if the battle itself had paused to take a breath.

Then, through some unheard command, flamelon warriors from around the battlefield suddenly turned, ran over, and attacked Basilgarrad. They swarmed over him, even as he squirmed to escape from the net. Shouting victoriously, they fanned out across the full length of his chest and tail and hacked mercilessly with their broadswords and spears. Yet the dragon's sturdy scales repelled all their blows; sword blades cracked and spears shattered.

"His eyes!" cried one canny captain, who realized that no scales covered the dragon's lids. "Pierce his eyes!"

Flamelon warriors started climbing up the net, working their boots into the gaps between the thick strands. Basilgarrad shook himself, trying to throw them off. But though he managed to toss some soldiers aside—and rock his body enough to crush a few under his bulk—every movement only tightened the cleverly woven strands. Soon he couldn't even budge his tail, legs, or head. The net squeezed his chest so hard that every breath grew more labored.

Again he roared, though now his voice sounded more like a long, painful moan. *How can this be? I'm trapped. Powerless!*

The flamelon captain, a burly warrior with muscular arms, was the first to reach one of the dragon's eyes. Its rich green glow bathed the warrior in magical light, but he didn't seem to notice. He merely braced his feet on the net, then started to raise his broadsword above his head, getting ready to plunge his blade deep into the unprotected flesh.

"I will blind you, cursed dragon!" he cried, lifting the sword higher.

Basilgarrad, once the most powerful creature in Avalon, could only watch the sword rising. Never, since he'd gained a dragon's body, had he felt so small. So weak. So utterly alone.

Now I'll never get to the Haunted Marsh, he thought somberly. With as much of a sigh as he could muster, he added, *And I'll never see Marnya again.*

A loud, rasping laugh shook him out of his thoughts. Recognizing that sound immediately, his whole body quaked with rage within the confines of the net. But knowing it would be one of the last sights he would ever see, he refused to look up at the sky. He couldn't bear to see the gloating face of Lo Valdearg.

"Well now, what do we have here?" sneered his foe,

swooping so low that Basilgarrad felt the fire dragon's hot breath on his ears. "A green worm. In a net!"

If I ever get free . . . , thought Basilgarrad, grinding his teeth.

"Right now," said Lo Valdearg between spurts of laughter, "you're probably thinking about what you'd like to do to me if you ever get free. Well, ease your little mind, Green. You'll never get free! *Never.*" With that, he laughed so hard that sparks rained down on the bound dragon and all the flamelons climbing on his body.

One of those sparks landed on the flamelon captain's brow at the very instant he was about to drive his sword down into the glowing eye. He paused, just long enough to bend his head to his shoulder to brush away the spark. Then he straightened, squeezed the hilt with both hands, and suddenly froze.

Basilgarrad watched, puzzled, as the captain's entire body tensed. The warrior's expression changed from wrath to shock. His rust red eyes opened to their widest. Then a sword blade exploded from his chest, rammed with such force that his armored chest plate burst apart.

The captain, still clutching his own sword, fell from his perch and tumbled down to the ground. On the spot where he'd been poised to strike, her straggly gray hair billowing in the wind, stood Babd Catha, the Ogres' Bane.

She nodded at the captive dragon, a satisfied glint in her eyes. Then she spun around and yelled, "Cut him loose, dwarves! I'll buy ye some time."

Instantly, she threw herself at a trio of flamelons who had climbed up to the dragon's snout to avenge their slain captain. With lightning fast strokes, she skewered one, lopped the head off another, and slammed the third on the brow with her hilt, so hard he keeled over unconscious. Not pausing for a second's rest, she flew into a whole new band of warriors, slashing and thrusting so forcefully that she cleared a wide area around the dragon's jaw.

Meanwhile, Basilgarrad saw more movement at the edge of his vision. A troop of dwarves, shielded by Babd Catha's onslaught, marched up to his jaw and started chopping at the net with their axes. Led by Urnalda, whose curly red locks still bore several strings of crystals, the dwarves hacked furiously at the thick strands.

"Stop them, you idiots!" roared Lo Valdearg. He swooped lower, wings pumping, and released a blast of flames. But he overestimated the dwarves' height, so his fiery breath barely grazed their heads—and struck instead a group of flamelon soldiers who were gathering to attack. The soldiers sprawled onto the ground, shrieking from their burning clothes and hair.

"Keep chopping!" Babd Catha shouted to the dwarves. She fought with as much energy as twenty warriors, spinning and striking constantly. But Basilgarrad noticed, to his horror, several deep gashes in her torso and legs. One broken blade still hung from her shoulder plate, not far from her neck. Blood oozed from the spot, staining her armor.

Lo Valdearg swung around again, flying straight at the dwarves. He drew a deep breath that would, he felt certain, incinerate these ax-wielding pests. Aiming lower this time, he started to exhale a blast—when a small object soared straight into his eye.

Shrieking in pain, Lo Valdearg spun out of control. With terrified flaps of his wings, he righted himself only an instant before crashing to the ground. Dazed and aching badly in his eye, he climbed slowly skyward. His uninjured eye scanned the air for whatever had flown into him. But he saw no trace of anything dangerous.

Far below him, a young, thin-winged dragon coasted down to rest on the branch of an old oak tree at the edge of the battlefield. His little lungs heaved from exertion, his wings throbbed, and his claws ached from scratching Lo Valdearg's eye so hard they almost broke. Yet Ganta couldn't keep himself from smiling. He had done something brave—maybe even something big.

A rip! Basilgarrad felt one strand loosen, ever so slightly, by his lower lip. He strained to open his jaws, while the dwarves' axes chopped away at more strands. Another one burst open with a loud *thhhwang*. Then another.

The dragon strained mightily to open his jaws, his whole head quivering. Yet too many strands still bound him tight. He could see, above him, the scarlet shape of Lo Valdearg circling for another attack.

Hurry! He moaned ardently to the dwarves. *Work faster!*

Babd Catha, meanwhile, was slowing down. She stumbled

and missed some thrusts, no longer able to hold back all the flamelons. Already, three of them had bolted past her, charging the dwarves. Urnalda stopped slashing at the net to protect her people from the warriors. Though much shorter than her enemies, she swung her ax like a whirlwind, keeping them at bay.

Mostly recovered, Lo Valdearg glared down at the green dragon who had caused him so much trouble. He knew this was his last chance to kill Basilgarrad. Only a few seconds remained, he could see with his one good eye, before his foe burst free of the net. Despite the risks, he would land on Basilgarrad's eyes and rip them out with his claws. Then—with great pleasure—he would breathe a blast of flames so powerful it would burn away his enemy's brain.

Basilgarrad glanced at the sky again just as Lo Valdearg dived. *He's attacking! And I still . . .*

He strained every muscle in his jaws, trying to break free.

Can't . . .

Harder he worked, and still harder.

Move.

For all his desperate effort, he still couldn't open his jaws! In just a few seconds, his nemesis would pounce on him, intending to kill, and he would be defenseless. Basilgarrad's mind whirled. *What can I do?*

Turning skyward again, his heart leaped—and then sank. Leaped, because he saw another dragon suddenly appear, bearing down on Lo Valdearg. Sank, because he recognized that dragon—smaller than her foe, flying awkwardly, and clearly not experienced as a fighter.

No, Marnya! Don't do this!

He could only think, not shout, those passionate words. For his jaws, like the rest of him, remained bound.

6: A DRAGON'S TEAR

Some say "The end is near," as if that is somehow shocking news.
The truth is, the end is always near. What is actually shocking
is that we, ourselves, can help to choose which end.

Marnya, seeing Basilgarrad's plight, flew into battle. Despite her lack of fighting experience and the fire dragon's superior size and strength, she didn't hesitate. For she did possess one valuable quality—fury. The dragon she loved, whose company she longed for, would surely die unless she intervened.

Spreading her long, sturdy flippers—narrower than wings but wide enough to support her body in flight—she dived headlong at Lo Valdearg. The deep blue scales on her back glistened like the waters of her home in the Rainbow Seas, though her azure eyes shone even brighter. Trying her best to steer, she opened the webbing on her flippers' edges to their widest, just as Basilgarrad had taught her.

Seeing her approach, Lo Valdearg abruptly veered out of his dive to defend himself. His hated enemy was still bound in the net—and, judging from this new foe's slender frame and unsteady flight, it wouldn't take more than a few seconds to vanquish her. Then he could return to his primary goal: killing Basilgarrad.

He spun into attack position, stretching his wings for maximum agility. The hot furnace within his chest began to rumble. Only then did his uninjured eye notice something significant. This attacker was a water dragon!

"How is that possible?" he puzzled aloud. Then, shaking his huge head, he added, "No matter. Now she will die!"

Far below, Basilgarrad cringed. *No, Marnya! Turn back. He will destroy you!*

Frantically, he tried again to open his jaws. He threw every fiber of his being into the task, shaking with effort. His eyes felt ready to pop out of his head. But the thick strands held tight. Dwarves continued to hack at them with their ax blades—though not fast enough.

Desperately, he glanced around for any possible source of help. Yet no help existed. His remaining allies couldn't do any more than what they were doing now—fighting for their lives. Urnalda, swinging her heavy ax wildly, would not be able to hold back the flamelons much longer. And the great warrior Babd Catha showed growing weakness. She wobbled unsteadily after every new thrust or parry, while her foes slashed at her mercilessly.

Basilgarrad turned back to the sky, and what he saw struck more deeply than a battle wound. Marnya was charging Lo Valdearg head-on! But by flying straight at her foe as he hovered, she unwittingly gave him the opportunity to blast her with superheated flames. Without the advantage of élano-hardened scales, as Basilgarrad possessed, she would surely die. Most painfully.

As Marnya drew closer, the fire dragon's chest rumbled louder. Smoke started to pour from his nostrils. He waited until the precise instant she flew into range, clawing at the air with anticipation. Then, drawing a deep breath, he opened his enormous mouth and . . .

Roared with rage! Just as he prepared to blast his foe, Marnya shot a blast of her own. Jets of blue ice exploded from her nostrils, slammed into his wide-open mouth, and instantly doused his flames.

The impact knocked Lo Valdearg backward. Even as he struggled to right himself, blue ice clogged his mouth and throat, making him gag. Sputtering with wrath, he smashed his jaws together, splintering chunks of ice with his teeth. He spat out the remains, more eager than ever to demolish this foe.

He whirled around, facing Marnya with vengeful slashes of his claws. This time, she wouldn't outwit him! And she would feel every agony possible before she died. He charged, wings beating furiously.

Basilgarrad, watching from below, felt a surge of relief at Marnya's clever tactic. He wanted to cheer her success, but the only sound he could make through his lashed jaws was a vigorous moan. Then, seeing Lo Valdearg's angry charge, his moan became a whimper. Marnya was about to die! The warrior dragon would soon maul her, tearing her to shreds with his claws.

With all his might, Basilgarrad tried to open his jaws. He worked every last muscle even as, high above, Lo Valdearg shot straight at Marnya. Knowing that only seconds remained, the great green dragon writhed in the net, straining as never before.

Thhhwang. A strand broke!

Then another. And another, followed by an entire row. Dwarves, wielding their axes, shouted jubilantly as Basilgarrad opened his jaws a crack. Harder he strained. The crack widened. More strands frayed, then broke.

All at once, the net burst apart. Strands exploded into the air. Basilgarrad opened his jaws and roared with all the power of a dragon unleashed.

Moving with lightning speed, he bit through the net holding his legs, wings, and tail. The torn net lay across his back like a blanket, but it no longer bound him. He shook violently, tossing the huge net onto his tail. Then he braced himself, arched his mighty back, and hurled the net high into the sky.

Lo Valdearg, only a wing's length away from his prey, raked at the air with his claws. Marnya, unsure what else to do, faced him bravely as he charged, knowing she couldn't possibly evade such an attacker. She tried to blow another blast of ice, but with so little time to recover, she couldn't produce more than a few small shards.

An instant before the fire dragon's claws slashed her face,

a huge net flew into him from below. Lo Valdearg screeched in sudden panic as the net struck. Thick strands wrapped around his wings and neck, tangling him completely.

Rolling helplessly in the air, he shot past Marnya. She quickly tilted her flippers just enough to avoid getting entangled herself as he tumbled by. Then, relieved, she watched as the scarlet dragon plunged down, down, down. He released one last scream of terror, a cry that echoed in the air like an anguished wind, then crashed headfirst onto the battlefield. The troop of flamelons he crushed never knew what hit them.

Basilgarrad, too, watched his enemy's fall. He felt a surge of satisfaction when Lo Valdearg screamed, and an even greater one when he heard the unmistakable snap of the fire dragon's neck. Yet that feeling paled compared to his joy at the sight of Marnya, alive and well, soaring through the sky.

Before he could celebrate with her, however, he had work to do. Turning to the flamelons who had ensnared—and nearly killed—him, Basilgarrad exploded into action. With one scoop of his wing, he captured the warriors battling Urnalda, ground them roughly together, and hurled their remains beyond the borders of the realm. Then he slammed his terrible jaws on a score of flamelons who were still jabbing ruthlessly at the wounded Babd Catha. An instant later, he swallowed most of the others who had so recently swarmed over his body.

The few soldiers who escaped the wrathful dragon's jaws ran away, tripping over themselves to escape. At the same time, surviving flamelons all around the battlefield grasped the bitter truth. Their invasion, so certain to be victorious at the outset, had failed. Catastrophically.

As if they suddenly smelled that fact on the breeze, flamelons began a hasty retreat. Soldiers by the dozen broke ranks and ran off, stumbling into the neighboring forests, often pursued by an angry centaur or a band of elven archers. Only a few moments after Lo Valdearg had crashed to the ground, the battlefield was nearly empty of attackers.

Despite their vastly superior numbers, training, and weaponry, the invading armies had gained only a bloodbath. Scattered across the meadows, pristine just yesterday, lay piles and piles of dead flamelon soldiers and fire dragons. Although many of the defending fighters had also died, they had battled with such vigor and courage that many others had survived.

Basilgarrad scanned the battlefield, still grieving for the losses but also proud. Really proud—of the people who had bravely thrown themselves at this overwhelming enemy, motivated not by greed and vengeance but by love. For their homes, their freedom, their world. *Maybe*, he thought, *they weren't so foolish after all.*

He sensed, too, that this battle had finally broken the ugly alliance between the warlike flamelons and the jewel-hungry fire dragons. That it could well have ended the agony of the War of Storms, leaving only the monster in the Haunted Marsh to be confronted. And that its fiery combat in the sky and on the ground would make it famous in the ballads of wandering bards. *The Battle of Fires Unending,* he mused, *would make a good name.*

Glancing at the sky, he saw Marnya descending. Her long, sturdy flippers rode the air with ease; she'd certainly improved from that first awkward lesson outside her father's lair. As she approached, her azure blue eyes outshone even his memory of them.

Then he heard a painful moan nearby. Babd Catha! The old warrior, her gray hair splattered with blood, lay on her back, sword by her side. Her body, riven with gashes, trembled with every breath.

Quickly, he swung his snout to her side. She looked directly up into his enormous face, meeting his gaze with her own. Fire still burned in her dark brown eyes, undiminished by pain and loss of blood.

"Dragon," she said gruffly, "ye should've let me finish off them soldiers. I had them on the run."

Taken aback, Basilgarrad blinked his huge eyes in surprise. Part of him wanted to grin at her feisty nature, while most of him wanted to ease her agony. "I know," he said at last, "but I decided to end their misery. You would have been far less merciful."

Pleased with his response, she chortled hoarsely. But the laugh quickly turned into a cough, brutal and violent. Flecks of blood splattered her cracked lips. After a long moment, the coughing finally ended, leaving her chest heaving and her fire considerably dimmed.

"How can I help y—"

"Dragon," she sputtered, cutting him off, "I want ye to live. Aye, live! An' fight some more fer Avalon."

"I will," his deep voice rumbled. "But can I help you somehow? I can't heal you with magic, like Merlin. The only magic I know is how to cast smells, and that's utterly useless! Maybe, though, there is something I can do."

"Jest live," she declared, her wrinkled brow quivering. "This was a good battle to die. A proud last battle." She started to cough, but fought it back. "Fer me, but not fer you! This place, this world, dragon . . . it needs the likes of us. Warriors who would rather . . . live in peace."

Basilgarrad blinked again, trying to clear the clouds from his vision. "But who," he added, "will fight to the death to protect our friends."

The old warrior's hand, moving feebly, wrapped around the hilt of her sword. "Not jest our friends. Our beautiful world. Our bold idea."

Our bold idea, he repeated silently.

After a long pause, he answered, "I will, Babd Catha. I will live and fight." His massive lips turned up slightly. "Though not as well as you."

She grinned for an instant, then convulsed in a wave of pain. It took several seconds for her to catch her breath again. When she spoke, her voice rasped, and she paused often to lick her parched lips.

"There is one . . . more thing," she said weakly. "One favor I'll ask of ye."

"Whatever it is, I'll grant it."

She drew a ragged breath. "See that I'm buried up north . . . in the high peaks. In the deep snow." A subtle gleam lit her face. "Ye see, I've always loved . . . the snow."

Babd Catha, the Ogres' Bane, closed her eyes for the last time. And though her lips had been dry, they were now moistened by a dragon's tear.

7: SOMETHING IS COMING

*Sometimes, when I wonder what lies over the horizon, I wish
that a horizon could be not just an edge . . . but a barrier.*

Marnya landed on the battlefield, spraying mud and tufts
of grass as she slid to a stop. Seeing Basilgarrad, head
bent over the dying Babd Catha, she walked slowly to his side.
She watched, in silence, as the two great warriors for Avalon
spoke their final words. Then, as the green dragon shed a
tear, she gently placed her long blue flipper across his neck.

Slowly, Basilgarrad lifted his head and turned to her. Their
huge eyes met: one pair azure blue, sparkling like the deepest
sea; one pair radiant green, pulsing with the magic of Avalon.
In that shared gaze, much was said without words—about the
loyalty of friends, the brevity of life, the resilience of love.

Finally, Basilgarrad spoke, frowning sternly. "You were
terribly foolish to come, you know."

"Yes, I know," Marnya replied, resisting a grin. "But no
more foolish than you, trying to teach a water dragon how
to fly."

He tried to keep his frown, but it melted into a smirk. "I
had an especially challenging student." He chuckled, deep in

his massive throat. "Besides, that was the only way I could win the wager with your father."

Marnya's expression suddenly darkened, and she breathed a dragon-size sigh.

"Your father? He's not well?"

She gazed at him, her azure eyes glistening. "He is dead. Killed in an uprising to steal his throne."

"Killed?" Basilgarrad's nostrils flared angrily. "Who dared to do that?"

She slid her flipper off his neck and slammed it on the ground. Several flamelon helmets and discarded swords, lying on the grass nearby, jumped into the air from the vibration. "His royal guards," she answered, "led by the son of that one with the scarred snout you fought."

The green dragon's whole body shook with rage. He clawed viciously at the turf, gouging deep trenches.

"They made a secret pact with the fire dragons, who promised all sorts of jewels and precious crystals. He fought bravely, and killed most of them . . . but he died from his wounds."

"All because he refused to join the fire dragons' army and go to war."

Marnya nodded her great blue head. "He told me, more than once . . ." She stopped to swallow. "That he would never go to war with you on the other side. Because he respected your wisdom too much. And also, I think, because he feared your wrath too much."

Basilgarrad grimaced. "Bendegeit, the greatest highlord

who ever ruled the water dragons, feared nobody's wrath. Nobody's."

She looked at him soulfully, but said nothing.

"And as to my wisdom," he added with a shake of his head, "in that he was just plain wrong. You couldn't fill an ogre's ear with all the wisdom I have."

"Not true," she protested. "Without your wisdom and courage, there would be no Avalon left. Everyone knows that."

Basilgarrad peered at her. "What everyone *doesn't* know is what a colossal idiot I am! Why, just before you arrived, I almost forgot about . . . well, the Avalon idea. I started to believe, really believe . . ."

"What?"

"That I was alone." His gaze roamed across the battlefield—the body of brave Babd Catha, the hundreds more bodies of fallen fighters, the celebrating dwarves and men and women, the scattered groups of grieving elves, the lifeless hulk of Lo Valdearg, and even the small winged dragon clinging to the branch of an oak tree. "All alone."

She tapped the charred scales of his shoulder with her flipper, knocking a boulder-sized chunk of charcoal to the ground. "You must have been discouraged, very discouraged." Her azure eyes brightened. "But, my love . . . you were never alone."

He peered at her in silence. And he understood—for the first time in his entire life, it seemed—how right she really was.

Marnya peered back at him. Then her long, slender tail

undulated on the ground, sweeping aside several fallen flame-lons and a broken beam from the tower that had so nearly caused his death. In a joyful tone, she said, "Now that this final battle is over, and the enemies all defeated, people can go back to living in peace!"

Sidling closer, she nuzzled against his neck. "Including," she added softly, "two dragons who have lived apart much too long."

Basilgarrad's whole immense body quivered with delight at her words. But his expression quickly darkened. "This battle, important as it was, isn't the final one. At least . . . not for me."

The water dragon tensed and pulled away. "Not final? Who is left for you to fight?"

"A monster who serves Rhita Gawr. Who has done eve-rything possible to cause misery and havoc. And who is hid-ing in . . ."

He hesitated, not happy to say the words. "The Haunted Marsh."

"The Marsh?" She looked at him, aghast. "*Nobody* goes there."

"I must. Or all the sacrifices people have made," he said with a nod toward Babd Catha's lifeless body, "will have been wasted."

"What are you planning to do there?"

"Whatever it takes," he answered grimly, "to stop—"

Marnya suddenly gasped. Staring at the sky behind him, she asked, "What in the name of dragons' blood is *that*?"

Basilgarrad swung his immense head. He gnashed his

teeth and began to growl deep in his throat. For he saw what she had seen in the sky—an ominous cloud, darker than night, flowing over the horizon. But what kind of cloud? It wasn't rain or snow . . . or, indeed, anything natural. The way it moved, grasping like a ghostly hand as it drew nearer, was unlike any cloud he'd ever seen.

He sniffed the air, opening his nostrils to their widest. Instantly, his brow creased, forming long trenches between the scales.

"What is it?" demanded Marnya, still watching the perilous cloud.

"Something rancid, even poisonous. Full of dark magic, I'll wager." He sniffed again, grateful for his powerful sense of smell—which, unlike his ability to make new smells, proved occasionally useful. "It smells like something . . . familiar. Something I've met before. Long ago."

"What?"

"I'm not sure." He stiffened from the tip of his snout to the end of his tail. "But it's coming from due east. The direction of the Haunted Marsh."

"Look!" cried a young elf nearby. "On the horizon. Something is coming!"

Other voices started shouting, swelling into a frenzied chorus. Women and men, hawks and bears, dwarves and elves all trained their eyes on the ominous cloud.

Marnya moaned with dread.

Her mate sniffed the air again, his mind whirling. Where had he encountered that smell?

"What *is* it?" repeated Marnya.

"Leeches!" exclaimed Basilgarrad. "Flying leeches—a huge swarm. There must be thousands and thousands of them."

He drew a deep dragon's breath. "I don't know what power they have, but it's deadly. I can feel it. And they're coming fast. I must stop them! Before they get here."

Desperately, he faced Marnya. "And you—you must go. Now!"

She swallowed, staring straight at him. "No. I will stay here with you."

"But you—"

"Will stay," she vowed. "With you. I've lost too much time with you already."

Basilgarrad studied her pleadingly, but could tell she wouldn't change her mind.

"All right, then," he said somberly. "We must find some way to stop them."

"How?"

Anxiously, he thumped his gargantuan tail on the ground. "I don't know, Marnya. I truly don't know."

8: THE SWARM

Trouble has many siblings. And like most siblings, they usually appear when you least expect them.

Startled by the darkening sky, a flock of golden aurabirds suddenly flapped their wings in alarm. Light, warm yellow in color, shone from each of their radiant feathers, making every bird glow like a miniature star. Together, they rose skyward in a great rustle of wings, leaving their perches on the fragrant boughs of a cedar grove at the eastern edge of Woodroot.

Although they took flight at least twenty leagues away from the muddy battlefield where Basilgarrad and Marnya now stood watching the sky, the dragons could easily see the glowing flock. The birds lifted higher, a golden cloud that rose gracefully into the air, exemplifying the endless wonders of this world. Normally, viewing such a spectacle would be a rare delight. But for the dragons, it was a moment of horror.

"They're flying right into the swarm!" cried Marnya, clawing the ground as she watched.

Basilgarrad didn't answer aloud. Yet his thoughts screamed, *They're going to die! I don't know how, but I'm sure of it.*

Even as he thought those words, part of the dark swarm separated to reach for the aurabirds. Like an eerie tentacle of blackness, it stretched toward the flock, moving faster than the birds could fly. Both dragons, watching the horrifying scene, held their breath. The dark tentacle spread out as it approached its fleeing prey, surrounded the birds, then squeezed tighter in a death grip.

Basilgarrad roared in anguish. He watched, unable to prevent this slaughter, as the evil leeches attacked. He could see well enough to watch the birds' magical light vanish when dozens of leeches landed on them and bit their eyes, wings, breasts, and tails. Almost instantly, the lightless gray birds dropped dead to the forest below, falling like a somber rain.

The leeches, meanwhile, flew back up to rejoin their ghastly swarm. As they did so, the lone red eye on each flashed simultaneously, staining the sky the color of blood. Only seconds after the attack, the swarm reunited. All the while, it moved steadily closer to the battlefield.

"They sucked the life right out of those poor little creatures," said Marnya, speaking slowly because of the shock of what she'd just witnessed.

"They would do the same to big creatures, too," rumbled Basilgarrad. "Even creatures as big as us. My guess is they're the minions of that monster in the Marsh, bred to attack any mortal creature—including a dragon."

"How then," she demanded, "can you possibly fight them? Shouldn't we just try to escape? Maybe we could outfly them."

"Maybe we could." He slammed his heavy tail onto the

ground. "But none of these other people, our smaller friends who fought so bravely today, could do that. They would surely perish . . . unless I can buy them time to escape."

"But if you try to fight those evil beasts"—she hesitated, flicking her ears at the swarm—"you will die."

His gaze locked on to hers. "Perhaps," he said gently. "And our future, what we might have had together—that, too, could die."

"What about Avalon?" she protested. "What about everything that will be lost if that monster prevails? If you die . . . who will be left to protect us?"

"I don't know, Marnya. But I do know that if I don't try to stop those minions and kill as many as I can, then nobody will be left at all! I must try—even if it costs my life."

She frowned, rippling the glistening blue scales of her neck. "Then let's fight them together."

"Are you sure?"

"Yes. Let's show them what we've got."

Feeling her resolve, he nodded. "And what we've got . . . is a lot."

The dark swarm, now so close it blackened almost half the sky, was nearly upon them. From every part of the meadows where that day's battle had been fought came howls and shouts and shrieks of fear. Many bold warriors who had survived the onslaught of the flamelons and fire dragons, who had overcome deadly weapons and grievous wounds, traded dire looks with their companions. Had they suffered so dearly and finally triumphed—only to die from this new wickedness?

One by one, with gathering speed, these warriors started to panic. They turned and ran, dropping their swords or spears—or worse, the hands of wounded companions. One man dashed into the forest, sprinting so fast he knocked down a pair of women who were themselves hobbling toward the trees. An elf maiden shrieked at the blackening sky so full of malice, then took her own dagger and plunged its blade into her chest. Bears scattered, loping toward the woods, along with men, women, and elves.

Only the centaurs, grim and proud, didn't panic. They merely stood facing the ominous sky, their hooves anxiously stamping the muddy ground. Among the few others to stay in place, as so many people succumbed to fear, was Urnalda, the leader of the dwarves. She stood erect, leaning against her battle-ax, as the gathering wind stirred her hair, clinking the quartz crystals. Another warrior who remained was young Ganta. Although his small teeth chattered at the sight of the approaching leeches, the little dragon clung firmly to his branch. As long as the great green dragon he admired chose to stay, he would do the same.

Seeing the growing mayhem on the battlefield, Basilgarrad raised his huge head and roared mightily. So loud was this blast that many people nearby toppled over from the sheer force of it. Most others on the muddy meadow stopped running away. Even some men, women, and elves who were just about to enter the trees halted and turned around.

As the wind, stirred by the poisonous swarm, swept across the battlefield, the dragon spoke. Eyes bright and voice strong, he called out, "Friends! Do not run away. Do not lose your courage. You are much too brave to panic!"

He drew a deep breath, filling his enormous lungs. "Our only hope to defeat this new enemy is to stay together. Fight together. Otherwise, we will surely die, each of us alone."

His throat rumbled as he lowered his voice a little. "If we must die today, then let us die side by side. Not scattered to the winds, each of us separated. No! Let us end this day as we began—joined together for Avalon."

He thumped his tail on the ground, sending tremors in all directions. "The truth, my friends, is that any one person, even a big person, is limited in size. But a people—a people with a shared purpose—can be infinitely large. And infinitely powerful."

All around him, heads began to nod. People gazed grimly at each other, or at the sky, but no longer at the false refuge of the trees. They understood that, if their lives had any worth on this terrible day, they would find that worth together.

Basilgarrad, having quelled the panic, turned back to the darkening sky. He knew that he and Marnya would attack this new enemy in just a few moments. They would fight, and die, courageously. It would be, in Babd Catha's words, *a good battle to die, a proud last battle.*

Yet as he watched the vile swarm approaching, he felt a great pang of sorrow. *Darker than dark.* That was the phrase that described the monster of the Marsh, and it also described the plans of its master, Rhita Gawr, to conquer Avalon. Now, as the deadly swarm arrived, he could do nothing to foil those plans and end this madness.

He looked again at Marnya. He saw in her face both courage and loyalty. As well as love. But not the slightest hint of hope. That did not surprise him, since he felt no hope himself.

Shadows from the sky darkened his brow. "All right," he declared, certain he would never say these words again. "It's time to fly."

Basilgarrad spread his wings, so wide they reached almost across the battlefield. He clenched his massive jaws and tensed his legs to leap into the sky. Marnya, he knew, would follow right behind—and their deaths, he knew also, would come soon after that. His claws dug deep into the turf as he started to spring.

"No need to do that, old chap."

The dragon started, then whirled around. That voice! Could it be?

Sure enough, he found himself facing an old friend. It was someone who had seen even more adventures than he had, someone who had a special knack for surprises.

Basilgarrad studied the friend in disbelief. "Hello, Merlin."

9: ILLUMINATION

What good are eyes, without the will to see? And what good is that will, without the light to see by?

"Hello, Basil."

Merlin, wearing a long blue robe whose seams had been embroidered with silver stars, peered at the dragon. His coal-black eyes sparkled. His gnarled staff, too, seemed to glow. While he couldn't be sure, Basilgarrad thought that one place in particular—the rune of a dragon's tail, carved into the shaft—glowed extra bright.

"Well, now," the wizard said with breezy casualness, "has anything new happened since I left?"

"Anything new!" bellowed Basilgarrad, loud enough to blow off the wizard's hat.

Tall, pointed, and severely crumpled, the hat fell to the ground at Merlin's feet. As he bent down to retrieve it, something stirred within the hairs of his bushy beard. Out from the middle of the beard, about halfway down the wizard's chest, emerged a small gray head, tufted with feathers, with two bright yellow eyes and a perilous beak.

"An owl!" said Marnya, stretching her neck to look more

closely. "I've always wanted to see one." Still thunderstruck by Merlin's sudden appearance, she kept shifting her gaze from the wizard to the owl and back.

"Yes, yes, an owl," said Merlin, picking up his hat. "And a rather willful one, at that."

Using the tip of his finger, he pushed the owl's head back into the folds of his beard. Now more gray than black, the beard provided perfect camouflage for the owl's feathers. Now stay there, Euclid, until I tell you it's safe to come out."

From deep inside his beard came the sharp *clack* of the owl's beak.

Jauntily, Merlin replaced his hat. Then, turning back to Basilgarrad, he asked, "Now, what were you about to say?"

"That you are as maddening as ever!" answered the dragon. His long ears swiveled. "But we'll talk about that later. Right now, we must deal with something more serious."

Basilgarrad glanced up at the approaching swarm of deadly leeches, so thick they blackened much of the sky. Now less than one league away, they were closing in fast. Already the strange whirring sound of their flight—as well as their rancid odor—had reached the battlefield. All around Merlin and the dragons, the warriors whom Basilgarrad had so recently calmed started to stir nervously. Many uttered prayers to the gods Dagda and Lorilanda; an equal number fingered their weapons, although they knew that mere blades wouldn't help against this enemy.

"Ah, yes," said the wizard, following the dragon's gaze. "I suppose we ought to deal with that."

Basilgarrad started to nod emphatically, until the wizard spoke again.

"That smell, I mean. Quite dastardly! Like curdled milk, only worse."

"Not just the smell," snapped the dragon. "Those evil leeches!"

"Hmmm, I see." Merlin peered at the sky. "They do look troublesome."

Even as he spoke, the sky darkened significantly. Shadows deepened across the battlefield, the remains of the fallen, and the anxious faces of all those who had survived. A chill wind swelled, sweeping over everyone. The whirring sound grew louder, the odor more noxious.

"Right!" bellowed Basilgarrad. "But how do we stop them? Those leeches will suck the life out of anyone they touch!"

"Quite so," agreed Merlin, seeming to be no more perturbed than if the dragon had pointed out a loose thread on his robe. "Before I tend to that matter, however, I want you to introduce me to your friend."

"My *what*?" Basilgarrad, frustrated to the breaking point, slammed his tail into the turf.

"Your friend there." The wizard gestured with the handle of his staff. "The one with the marvelously blue eyes."

"I am Marnya," she said, not waiting for Basilgarrad to calm himself enough to introduce her. "And I'm pleased to meet you."

"The pleasure is all mine, my dear." He gave a slight bow, all the while holding his finger over his beard in case Euclid decided to pop out again.

Turning to Basilgarrad, the wizard said calmly, "Now, then, with the introductions behind us, we can take care of business." He waved a hand at the blackened sky, now teeming with leeches. "What shall we do about them?"

"Whatever we can!" roared the dragon. "They'll be here in seconds!" He clawed the ground. "I'm going to attack them, unless you have a better idea."

"So will I," declared Marnya.

The wizard's eyes seemed to shine brighter than ever, despite the darkening shadows that covered everyone. "That won't be necessary."

Suddenly grim-faced, Merlin grasped his staff with both hands. He lifted it up, then forcefully jammed its tip into the ground by his feet. Holding tight to the shaft, he peered at it, concentrating his thoughts, then began to chant.

> *Fire of light,*
> *Fire of life—*
> *Brighten the darkness,*
> *Ending our strife.*
> *Break binding shadows,*
> *Barriers rife—*
> *Illumination:*
> *Fire of life.*

Glancing up at the dragons, he said, "If I were you, I'd close my eyes." Then, turning back to the staff, he spoke one simple command:

"Now."

In one instantaneous flash, thousands of thin beams of light shot out of the staff. *Zzzzzaaapp!* Like an exploding star, the light burst forth—with every single beam directed at one of the minions overhead.

Skewered by the light beams, the leeches died instantly. Their whirring noise abruptly ceased. Whatever crude intelligence they might have possessed, whatever hatred for their master's enemies they carried—all that vanished. They dropped out of the sky, falling like terrible, nightmarish rain. Their lifeless bodies fell onto the forests and meadows below, making a crunching sound as they struck, spotting the ground with their dark remains.

For a long moment, no one uttered a sound. The world fell quiet. In time, a gentle breeze moved through, rustling the leaves of the trees, carrying away the rancid smell. And then, as one, the survivors cheered. They raised their voices in shouts, brays, chirps, screeches, howls, hoots, and—in the case of Basilgarrad and Marnya—resounding roars.

Jubilation bloomed on the battlefield. Warriors raised their arms to the sky, cheering with all their hearts. Men and women embraced, elves danced, dwarves followed the lead of Urnalda and spun joyous circles around their axes. Even the surviving bears rolled exuberantly on the grass, kicking their burly legs and waving their paws. And in a tree at the far side of the battlefield, one little dragon whooped in delight, spread his wings, and flew over to be nearer to Basilgarrad.

Merlin allowed himself a grin of satisfaction. With the palm of his hand, he patted the top of his staff. Quietly, he said, "Well done, old friend."

Lifting his face, his gaze met Basilgarrad's. For the first time in many years, they heard each other's thoughts.

Nice work, offered the dragon, bending his ears toward the wizard. *But it took you long enough to get here.*

Yes, well, I met a few distractions on the way. A young and headstrong king tromping off to find the Holy Grail, a palace revolt, and a sorceress who tried to entrap me in a cave—the usual sort of thing. Nothing extraordinary. The wizard sighed and said aloud, "But I made it here, at last."

"That you did," agreed the dragon. "With your usual dramatic entrance."

Merlin chuckled, then his expression became serious. "I hope," he said softly, "that the losses haven't been too great."

Basilgarrad's silent stare said everything.

"I am sorry, Basil. Deeply sorry." He drew a long, slow breath. "Just as I arrived, though, I heard what you said to the others here. An excellent speech, with some hard-won wisdom."

"Too hard-won," answered the dragon solemnly, his gaze roaming across the field strewn with bodies. "Many people, too many, have died to protect Avalon. From the smallest of faeries to"—he paused to trade a glance with Marnya—"to the greatest of dragons."

"I know," said Merlin, eyeing the corpse of Babd Catha on the ground. "That is one fallen warrior who fought bravely, I'm sure."

"Most bravely." Basilgarrad's nostrils flared. "She must have felled two hundred invaders."

"And wished," Merlin added fondly, "for two hundred and one."

"And all she asked," added Marnya with a wave of her flipper, "was to be buried in the high peaks, under the snow."

"Snow?" sputtered Merlin. "But she *hated* snow, at least according to the bards."

"They were wrong." The dragon moved his snout closer, so that his nose practically touched Merlin's robe. "Now that you're back, we have work to do. Important work."

The wizard's white eyebrows, as fluffy as clouds, lifted. "Tell me, Basil."

"We must go to the Haunted Marsh! A shadowy beast lurks there, a monster known only as *darker than dark*." With the tip of his claw, he scraped some of the dead leeches on the ground. "It serves Rhita Gawr—and it certainly won't stop just because we've destroyed its minions."

Gravely, Merlin stroked his chin. "Who knows what other evil it could be planning? For us all—and for Avalon."

"You'll come, then? Even though all our efforts might not be enough?"

Merlin grinned. "Sounds like old times, my friend. Besides, as you know, even the smallest effort can matter." He twirled the hairs at the tip of his beard. "Long ago, I planted a certain seed, smaller than a pebble, with no idea—none at all—what it might become. A tiny, insignificant gesture at the time. But then the seed grew into this magical world, this chance to find peace at last."

He jabbed his staff into the ground. "We still have that

chance, Basil. Despite all that has happened." He drew a long breath. "And we must do whatever we can to keep it alive."

"What about Babd Catha?" asked Marnya. "We must heed her last request. That means a detour to the high peaks."

Basilgarrad sighed deeply. "You're right. But it will cost us time. Precious time."

"I will take her," declared a resolute voice.

All eyes turned to Urnalda, who had been listening to the conversation. She leaned against her ax handle, her squat frame as sturdy as ever despite the arduous battle she'd just fought. She nodded in greeting to Basilgarrad, Marnya, and Merlin, clinking the crystals in her hair.

"My people will pass near the high peaks on our way home," she explained. "It would be an honor to bear the body of such a great warrior."

Basilgarrad angled his ears toward her. "Thank you, my friend."

"It is I," she replied, "who should thank you. For all you have done today."

"All *we* have done," countered the dragon.

Merlin gave her a respectful bow. "Including you, Urnalda. Your grandmother, the first to bear your name, would be proud."

For the first time in that long day, the dwarf smiled. Then she spun on her boots and beckoned to her soldiers. Immediately, a dozen grim-faced dwarves strode to her side. They quickly made a stretcher from their cloaks and ax handles, gently lifted the body of Babd Catha, and marched away.

"Don't forget," called Basilgarrad. "In the snow."

Without turning around, Urnalda waved her stout arm in agreement.

The great green dragon faced Marnya. "Now, I'm afraid, we must—"

"Don't even think about it," interrupted the water dragon. Her azure eyes bored into him. "I am coming with you."

"But—"

She slammed her flippers on the ground for emphasis, spraying mud on both of their scales. "I am coming."

Basilgarrad knew he was beaten. "All right," he grumbled. "You win."

"Well done, lad," commented Merlin. "You're well on your way to a good life together."

Before the dragon could answer, another voice piped up. Though not so deep as Marnya's, it sounded equally determined.

"Me, too!" cried Ganta. His little body quaked with excitement as he scampered across the mud and skidded to a halt in front of the dragon he so greatly admired. "Please, master Basil, let me come with you."

"Absolutely not," roared his enormous uncle. "You have lived through a terrible battle today, and fought well. But I cannot allow you to risk your life again so soon."

"But, master Basil, I want to come!"

"No, Ganta. When you are older, perhaps. When you can breathe fire. Then I will take you."

"Please?"

"No!"

Ganta peered up at Basilgarrad and scrunched his little nose. "If you don't let me come, I'll just follow you anyway! You can't stop me."

The green dragon scowled at him, rumbling in his throat.

"Looks like stubbornness is a family trait, old chap." Merlin placed his hand on Basilgarrad's lower jaw. "He doesn't leave you much choice."

The dragon's eyes narrowed as he squinted down at Ganta. "So be it. You can come. But you must keep up with the rest of us."

"I will, master Basil, I will!" Ganta jumped up and down with excitement, splattering his small wings with mud.

Basilgarrad drew a dragon-size breath. He glanced at each of his companions, then declared: "All right. Time to fly."

10: MYSTERIES

Some questions must be answered. Others, though, should never be asked.

W ait!"

Merlin's command echoed across the battlefield. Marnya stiffened her back and flippers, while Ganta clacked his little teeth in surprise. At the same time, warriors across the corpse-strewn meadow jolted to attention. Centaurs, their horses' legs and haunches splattered with mud, turned to see what the wizard wanted. Elves, striding into the forest to return home, halted in midstep. An old eagle, perched on Lo Valdearg's lifeless tail, trained his golden eyes on the mage. A young woman, limping because of a gash on her thigh, stopped to watch.

But Merlin paid no attention to them. His gaze fell squarely on the one creature to whom he'd directed his command, the great green dragon beside him.

Basilgarrad stopped unfurling his wings, though they had already stretched far enough to shadow half the field. He shifted his massive bulk, grinding against the soil as if he were a mountain that could somehow pivot on its base. Slowly, he turned his head toward his friend. Their gazes met: The dragon's eyes, glowing green, peered into a coal-black pair that glittered with magic.

"Why?" demanded the dragon. "We must go! We can't afford to lose any more time."

Merlin merely stroked his long beard. From somewhere in the middle of the mass of gray hair came the sharp *snap* of an owl's beak. But the wizard didn't seem to notice.

"I understand," he said at last. "Yet we also can't afford to plunge into this new battle with no forethought." He twirled a strand of gray hair around his finger. "Just what do you know about this monster who sent the minions?"

"Precious little. Except that it smuggled itself into Avalon disguised as a leech." The dragon ground his spear-sharp teeth, recalling the leech's attempt, long ago, to kill him with malevolent magic. "And that it has grown steadily stronger, becoming so powerful it could attack us with this evil pestilence."

He swished the tip of his tail, hurling a dozen minion carcasses into the air. Two or three of them bounced off Merlin's blue robe. One hit the top of his shaft, which sizzled with sparks that instantly burned the carcass into ashes. And one grazed the side of Marnya's neck, making her rear up like a startled mare. She glared at the dead minion, growling angrily. Meanwhile, the scales on her neck turned shadowy gray for several seconds before finally returning to luminous blue.

Beneath his beard, Merlin scowled. "Anything else? Anything at all?"

"Only that it serves Rhita Gawr. And that its form is"—the dragon paused, recalling the shadowy image he'd first seen in Bendegeit's lair—"*darker than dark.*"

Merlin's fingers reached deeper into his beard, twirling ropes of hair. A sudden *snap* made him yelp and nearly jump out of his boots. He yanked his hand away from the beard, vigorously shaking a nipped finger.

"Now, Euclid," he scolded. "That was rude, brutal, and disgraceful! As well as positively unowlish." He frowned, examining his bruised fingertip. "Save your bites for mealtimes!"

From deep within his beard, muffled by all the hair, came a mirthful chuckling sound. Two yellow eyes gleamed mischievously, then disappeared in the gray strands.

Giving his finger another shake, Merlin turned again to the dragon. "All this is mysterious, Basil. Very mysterious."

"What do you mean?" The enormous tail thumped on the ground impatiently, spraying mud all around.

"I mean," replied the wizard, "that we have almost no idea what this monster is really like. Does it have any weaknesses? Why has it remained hidden for all this time? Does it have some more sinister plans, beyond defeating you and your allies in battle?"

"It serves Rhita Gawr!" roared Basilgarrad. "Do we need to know any more than that?"

"Yes, if we are going to defeat it." The tufted brows rose higher. "What I'd like to know most of all is . . . how exactly does it gain its power? From what source? What fuels all this"—he kicked a pile of minion carcasses—"this dark magic?"

The dragon slid his gargantuan head closer, so that his lower lip almost touched the point of Merlin's hat. In a low voice, he growled, "The only way we're going to find the answer is to go to the Haunted Marsh."

Merlin stroked the hair of his chin, keeping his hand well out of Euclid's reach. "That's another thing. Not a very hospitable place, that Marsh. I'd rather go any other place in Avalon! Even a goblin fortress is a pleasant destination by comparison. Just how do you know that's where this monster is hiding? What makes you so certain?"

"This," rumbled the dragon. Reaching up to his shoulder with a pair of claws, he plucked a small, charred scrap of paper from the gap above a scale. He then dropped the scrap, which twirled as it floated down into Merlin's open hand.

The wizard pursed his lips, studying the burned fragment. He pressed one finger against the hand-drawn arrow that remained visible. "I do sense magic here. Just a bare remnant, mind you, but enough to know that the magic was once very real, and also very strong. But what did this scrap come from?"

"A map. A magical map." Basilgarrad hesitated, remembering Merlin's severely damaged relationship with his son, Krystallus. "It was a gift from . . . a friend. Someone adventurous enough to have won it on his travels. And also generous enough to give it to me, because it could only be used once."

"And you used it to find where the monster is hiding?"

"I did. And it said, without any question, the Haunted Marsh."

Merlin nodded approvingly as he leaned against his staff, pushing its tip into the muddy ground. "That map was, indeed, a precious gift. A generous gift. What loyal friend of Avalon gave it to you?"

The dragon's broad chest expanded as he drew a deep breath. "Krystallus."

Merlin started, almost losing his grip on the staff. "Krystallus?"

"Yes. Your son."

Anguished wrinkles appeared on the mage's brow. "I have no son."

Basilgarrad gazed intently at his friend, knowing that this was not the time to discuss such a painful topic. In a firm but gentle tone, he rumbled, "We must go."

Merlin sucked in his breath. "Yes, you're right."

The wizard opened his hand, started to toss the scrap aside, then hesitated. For an instant he stared down at it, as if trying to read the mind of the person who had once owned it. Finally, with a somber shake of his head, he dropped the scrap and watched it float down to the mud.

"All right, then." Basilgarrad began to spread his wide wings again. "To the Marsh."

Marnya, too, opened her version of wings. Along the edges of both flippers, webbing expanded. Her gleaming blue tail pressed flat against the ground, ready to push hard enough to hurl her body into the sky.

By her side, near the splayed claws of one of her feet, young Ganta rustled his paper-thin wings. Tiny as they were, they dwarfed his slim body. In a small, piping voice, he cried, "I'm ready, master Basil. Let's win this fight for Avalon!"

The green dragon glanced down at his bold little nephew. "I hope we will, Ganta. I hope we will."

11: SHADOW OF A SHADOW

Of all the qualities of a survivor, the first and last are courage.

Far away from the battlefield where Basilgarrad and his companions had fought for their lives, a young hawk raced through a whirling sandstorm.

Like a silver-winged arrow, the hawk shot through gusts of blasting sand, ignoring all the tiny grains that pelted his feathers. Sand struck his eyes so forcefully he kept them almost shut, flying blind into the turbulent wind. Yet he continued to race through the swirling storm, his wings beating as fast as his heart.

For right behind him flew death.

Six vicious dactylbirds, their jagged wings slapping powerfully, shrieked with hunger. Every wingbeat hurled their bodies forward, as if they leaped across the air rather than flew through it. Their heavy-lidded eyes, dull red, stayed nearly closed, yet the hunters never veered from their prey. They could smell the blood of their victim through anything, even a cyclone of sand.

Their bloodstained talons slashed at the hawk. Murderously sharp, they raked the sky, just as they would soon tear through the feathers and flesh of this young bird who had dared to evade them. Once dactylbirds chose their prey, they almost always prevailed and gained satisfaction—even when that prey offered only a few bites of meat to chew on. Though hunger had sparked this pursuit, the predators now felt mostly bloodlust, made even greater by the hawk's desperate attempt to lose them in this howling storm over the desert of northern Malóch.

The dactylbirds shrieked louder than ever as their hooked beaks snapped just behind the hawk's tail feathers. Those feathers, like the silvery ones of the small bird's wings, showed terrible wear from this chase. Already, several torn pinions had fallen away, while many more showed rips and holes or were bent askew.

Desperately hoping to escape, the brave hawk flew speedily northward, right into the pelting sand. His tattered wings strained their hardest, though his muscles screamed with every stroke. He knew that his sole hope to survive lay in flying even deeper into this furious storm. Nothing else mattered. Not even the fact that his route was carrying him perilously close to the sinister place that lay just beyond the edge of this desert—a vile swamp so choked with deadly fumes and ghouls that people called it the Haunted Marsh.

At last, the hawk's bold gambit started to show success. He could hear the dactylbirds' shrieks grow quieter as they fell behind, at first only by a wing's length or two, then by more. Though he didn't dare to slacken his pace, let alone take the time to look behind, he sensed that his plan was working. He was going to live!

His wings beat harder, despite his strained muscles. Their strokes gained power from the taste of triumph, as well as his strong will to live. He could almost see, in his mind's eye, his mate, whose diamond-bright eyes and lively spirit had won his heart in the early days of spring. And he could almost hear the energetic peeping of the three healthy chicks who now filled their nest on a sheer cliff by the western coast of Mudroot.

When he'd first glimpsed the dactylbirds approaching, his only thought was to lure the predators away from his family. Now, however, he felt sure that he would also return home. A bit tattered from his escape, but very much alive.

As the distance between the hawk and his pursuers lengthened, the storm began to diminish. The winds didn't howl as loudly; the sand blew less forcefully. Spaces of relative calm appeared between the swirling gusts. Now and then he coasted on the swells, giving his exhausted wings a few seconds' rest. He even dared to open his eyes a little wider and caught his first glimpses of the desert dunes below.

The storm's fury faded, until finally he felt only occasional pecks of sand against his feathers. Finally, he chanced a look behind. Curling his neck, he opened his eyes fully and peered into the whirling cloud that he was leaving.

No sign at all of those miserable dactylbirds!

His chest swelled victoriously. He'd done the impossible. Not only had he saved his family, he'd eluded an entire flock of ruthless predators. He straightened his neck again—then noticed something strange.

A new and much darker cloud loomed straight ahead. Unlike the storm he'd just flown through, this cloud wasn't made of blowing sand. Nor was it made of dust or moisture or anything remotely tangible. No, this cloud was made from an eerie, concentrated essence that seemed, somehow, darker than a shadow of a shadow.

The hawk shuddered, then tilted his wings to veer away. From somewhere below, he heard a high, rasping shriek. He turned even more sharply. As he did, he caught a whiff of something putrid, as foul as a swamp of decaying corpses.

The Haunted Marsh!

With all his remaining strength, he beat his wings to fly away. He'd go anywhere, plunge back into the sandstorm if necessary—whatever it would take to get away from this frightful place. New power came to his strokes as he flew as fast as he could.

But not fast enough. At the instant the hawk veered away, something stirred within the dark cloud. A wispy shape, some sort of being that had no wings yet moved with alarming speed, rose out of the vapors, reaching swiftly toward him. Higher it stretched, and higher, like a shadowy hand, its vaporous fingers groping for its victim.

The hawk screeched in terror as the air around him suddenly darkened. At the same time, the temperature dropped sharply, chilling so much he felt the marrow of his bones begin to freeze. His muscles tightened, his sight disappeared, and no matter how hard he fought to escape this sinister grip, his strength faded.

He released one last muffled screech as a final thought filled his mind. How he knew this, he couldn't be sure. Yet he knew it beyond any doubt.

He'd been captured by a ghoul, one of the most feared residents of the Haunted Marsh.

12: A PRECIOUS MORSEL

Have you heard people say that we are what we eat? What we most consume? That's only partly true. What we truly are, in our depths, is what we most desire.

Slowly, inexorably, the marsh ghoul's deadly grip tightened. Darkness and cold seeped steadily into the hawk, clogging his mind and choking his breath. Weaker and weaker he grew, until he couldn't struggle any longer.

All the hawk could feel was the terrible, bone-cracking cold. Everywhere. Like a limp bunch of feathers, he lay in the ghoul's grasp, his dying heart only barely beating.

The shadowy creature of the Marsh could have easily killed him right then. It would take only one small additional squeeze, one quick cold breath, to extinguish the last remaining flicker of life in this little bird. Yet the ghoul resisted, keeping that flicker alive, as it shrank back down into the Haunted Marsh.

Why? Not because this bird's living meat was something so special it was worth saving. And not because the bird would yield much in the way of food; those few shreds would make barely a swallow. While any fresh meat, even such a tiny amount, was desirable, a true delicacy in these harsh days in the swamp, the ghoul resisted consuming its prey for one simple reason. The bird belonged to someone else.

The marsh ghoul's master waited, even now, for this most recent victim. Writhing in its pit of death, a hole filled long ago with rotting corpses, the monster Doomraga expected its slaves to deliver every creature they captured. Immediately. No matter how small, no matter how miserable, those victims provided nourishment . . . although that nourishment came from a source other than flesh and bone.

Doomraga craved something far more precious. Not the mere body of creatures—but their pain, their sorrow, their ultimate despair. Indeed, it could barely recall the days when it had fed, like a common leech, on the blood of its prey. For many years now it had thrived, instead, on suffering. The more horrible, the better.

Anywhere in Avalon, far beyond the borders of the Marsh, wherever creatures suffered—there Doomraga found sustenance. That is why it had done so much to sow the seeds of hatred, greed, and arrogance in this world, sending its servants to coax the flamelons, fire dragons, and others to go to war. At long last, those seeds had sprouted, producing the War of Storms. Nourished by all that negative energy, Doomraga had grown immensely large—and immensely powerful. Strong enough to send a whole army of minions, only moments earlier, to destroy that cursed green dragon who continued to be such a nuisance. And, even better, strong enough to complete its final—and greatest—task.

First, however, it would dine on the suffering of the small bird a marsh ghoul had just caught. It would drink some fresh pain as the ghoul crushed the bird's wings, breaking every single bone one by one. Then it would extract even more pain by commanding the ghoul to gouge out the bird's eyes. Last of all, it would sip the bird's death throes while the ghoul tore off—slowly, carefully—every scrap of living flesh. Only then, when the creature's heart finally stopped from so much intolerable agony, would the meal be finished.

Doomraga, contemplating this tasty treat, quivered with anticipation. Its huge, bloated body writhed within its pit, squirming like a gigantic worm. Every other being in the Marsh, including the rest of the ghouls, watched it fearfully, and their fear gave Doomraga something more to consume.

It was easy for them to watch their master's movements. Despite the pervasive darkness of the Haunted Marsh, Doomraga remained clearly visible. And that was not because it glowed or produced any light besides the occasional flash of its single bloodred eye, although those flashes were so powerful they tinted the entire Marsh red for several seconds.

Rather, Doomraga could always be seen because it emitted a deeper kind of darkness, blacker than anything else nearby. For it had long ago become the utter darkness of the void. A being whose form was defined not by light . . . but by the total absence of light. A monster whose very flesh was the concentrated essence of night.

Its name, in the language of the spirit world, meant *darker than dark*. And that name fit its plans as well as its body, since

Doomraga itself was a slave to an even greater being, someone who hungered to conquer Avalon—and all other worlds, including that home of mortals called Earth.

Rhita Gawr. The immortal warlord of the spirit realm had tried many times to devour Avalon. Just as he had tried to devour Avalon's predecessor, the land called Lost Fincayra, in whose magical soil the Great Tree had sprouted. But never before had Rhita Gawr come so close to success—so close that he could now almost taste his ultimate triumph.

The time had come, both Doomraga and its master knew, to complete the final task. To begin the conquest of Avalon. But first, thought the monster of darkness, it would consume that precious morsel. Doomraga's massive form writhed within the pit, crushing the corpses beneath it. Anticipation bubbled out of its shadowy skin, coating its blackness like poisonous sweat.

Now it would dine on a small bird's painful death.

13: THE DARK THREAD

I knew the situation was dire and the time remaining was short. I just didn't know how dire. And how short.

The marsh ghoul glided back down to the swamp, its shadowy form clutching the limp body of the hawk. As it landed, splashing down in the putrid, reeking swamp, it gazed up at its master—and trembled with fear. Doomraga's vast, tubular body was now larger than ever . . . and darker than a hole in the night.

Sensing the arrival of its newest victim, some mortal creature who would provide a tasty sip of suffering, Doomraga quivered with pleasure. Up and down its great bulk, tremors rippled through the concentrated darkness. Then, from deep inside its core, came a hoarse, bone-chilling sound. Doomraga's laughter echoed across the Haunted Marsh, paralyzing every other creature, filling each with despair.

The laughter grew louder and more raspy—then suddenly stopped. For a long moment, nothing stirred. Nothing breathed. Every being in the Marsh kept absolutely still, as quiet as the corpses in Doomraga's pit.

All at once, the monster of darkness released a new sound.

But not laughter. Rather, Doomraga roared with uncontrollable rage, a terrible cry that was half bellow, half shriek. And entirely hateful.

Someone had destroyed its army of minions! Their lives, thousands and thousands of them, had all ended in an instant. Just as the monster had felt its minions' terrible power long after they had departed to destroy its enemies on the battlefield, it now felt that power suddenly vanish—as if a piece of its own dark heart had been brutally torn away.

Doomraga rocked back and forth on its bed of corpses, howling wrathfully, crushing whatever skulls and bones its weight hadn't already smashed. Anger boiled through its enormous body, along with a great sense of loss. How could its minions have died?

Suddenly, it stopped rocking. Rising to its full, towering height, Doomraga stood nearly motionless. Its only movement came from the dark surface of its body, which quivered like windblown water. Something new was in the air—a repugnant smell it hadn't detected in years.

Merlin! That miserable wizard, its greatest foe, had somehow returned to Avalon! On top of that, another familiar smell still rode the air—the stinking scent of the wizard's pet, that troublesome green dragon. That pest somehow remained alive!

The dark beast released another round of angry bellows. The hateful cries shook the swamp, so violently that dozens of marsh ghouls cowered and slunk away. Even the ghoul holding the limp hawk did its best to make itself small and inconspicuous. Though it wanted badly to retreat to the far side of the Marsh, it knew that trying to do so would mean certain death.

Questions clawed at Doomraga, making its red eye glow with rage. Why had Merlin chosen now, of all times, to reappear? Could he have possibly sensed the imminence of Doomraga's final task—and its importance for Rhita Gawr's triumph?

There were other irksome questions, too. Why was that cursed dragon so difficult to kill? What magic—or more likely, what luck—kept that foolish creature alive?

"Both of them must die!" roared Doomraga. Its cry tore through the Marsh like an angry wind, scattering noxious fumes, breaking the branches of dead trees, and blowing away frothy pools. "But first, something else must be born."

Once again, the monster started to rock back and forth. Its whole body shook violently, grinding its base into the Marsh. For a long-awaited time had arrived.

Before it would have the pleasure of destroying the wizard and the dragon, it would first perform a stunning feat. A feat it had labored long and hard to be ready to achieve. A feat that would ensure the conquest of Avalon.

Doomraga bent its vast bulk, then rose up vertically. Like a titanic tower of darkness it rose out of the Marsh, turning its lone eye toward the stars. The monster stood there, swaying, as it searched through the clouds of fumes rising from the Marsh, looking for one particular place in the sky. At last, it found the spot: a black gash that had once held the constellation called the Wizard's Staff, a group of stars that Rhita Gawr had caused to go dark.

The red eye flashed brighter than ever before, turning the whole marsh the color of blood. Then, from the darkened constellation on high, came an answering flash—equally red, equally terrifying. It lasted only an instant, but that was long enough.

Doomraga's final task was about to begin. And that meant, the monster knew well, Avalon's freedom was about to end.

It released another gargantuan roar, so loud that even the stars above seemed to tremble on high. This time, though, the roar came not from anger, but from sheer exertion. For Doomraga was delving into its deepest reserves of strength, calling on all its dark powers, to do what Rhita Gawr had commanded. That task would require every drop of its evil magic—magic that, like its own body, had swollen in proportion to Avalon's suffering.

Concentrating its power, the towering beast stood above the Marsh. Even before the echoes of its roar faded away, it started to make a new sound—a deep, rhythmic groan that throbbed with urgency. With every pulsation of the groan, ripples of darkness coursed through the monster's body, moving from its bloodshot eye down its full length to its base in the pit of corpses. Like a bloated worm rising vertically out of the swamp, it swayed ominously with every groan, every ripple of dark magic.

As it labored, vapors started rising out of the Marsh. They wrapped themselves slowly around Doomraga's body, growing thicker with each vibration. In time, they began to pulse with the same eerie rhythm, crawling over the monster's skin like ghostly serpents.

At the same time, the marsh ghouls lifted themselves out of hiding and encircled their master. They swirled around its midsection, their shadowy forms moving in a frightful dance. To the rhythm of their master's groans, they started to chant, repeating a single word over and over and over.

"DOOMraga, DOOMraga, DOOMraga, DOOM," they chanted. The relentless drumbeat of their voices pounded across the Marsh. "DOOMraga, DOOMraga, DOOM."

From the monster's inner core, halfway down its tubular form, a dark thread erupted. Slowly at first, then with gathering speed, the thread stretched skyward. Made from concentrated dark energy, it shot sparks of black lightning, crackling as it expanded.

The growing thread passed right through the ring of ghouls. They didn't slow their rotations or cease their chants, but merely shifted to allow the thread to pass. Higher and higher it stretched, reaching steadily toward the stars. Black sparks sprayed from its length and then fell into the Marsh, sizzling as they struck the rancid pools.

Beneath its rhythmic groans, Doomraga chortled with satisfaction. Everything about this thread was working just as Rhita Gawr had promised. And something else was working, too—something that no one else in Avalon yet understood.

Another thread of evil energy had emerged from one of the darkened stars of the Wizard's Staff, a star that was actually a passageway to the Otherworld of the Spirits. The realm of Rhita Gawr. Right now, as Doomraga's thread reached higher, the other thread stretched downward, growing even more rapidly. And when, before long, those two dark threads connected . . .

Doomraga's groans swelled louder. Partly from the added strength of anticipation, the taste of certain victory. And partly, as well, from the knowledge that with that victory would come the most delicious meal of all.

Revenge.

14: LUMINOUS MIST

Sometimes I can see most clearly when I close my eyes.

Y ou *what?*"

Serella's shout of dismay echoed around the mist-shrouded cliffs. Never one to hide her feelings, the proud queen of the elves stared, aghast, at her climbing partner.

Krystallus cringed. He took a step backward—a rather small step, since they were standing on a narrow ledge of rock that jutted out from the cliff wall. Not to mention the fact that the ledge was more than two thousand man-heights above the floor of the canyon.

"You what?" she repeated, even louder this time—so loud that pebbles broke loose and clattered down the rocky face. Although she was many leagues away from Avalon, in the distant world of Fincayra, her voice might have reached all the way to the Great Tree and stirred its highest branches. At least that was how it seemed to Krystallus, who backed up to the very edge of the ledge.

"Now, now," he protested, fidgeting with the climbing rope around his hips. "Let me explain."

"You've explained enough already." Serella glared at him,

her deep green eyes ablaze. "You gave away the map—the only one of its kind, the most magical map ever known! After all you went through to win it from that horrible old hag, Domnu—"

"Shhhhh," he interrupted her, shaking his head. "Don't throw her name around. This is her realm, you know. She could appear at any moment."

"I don't care," snarled the elf queen. "She could materialize out of these misty cliffs and it wouldn't bother me."

To emphasize her point, she slapped her open hand against the cliff wall, scattering the veil of mist that coated its surface—like every other surface in Lost Fincayra. Ever since this land had been saved by Merlin long ago, and had merged with the spirit realm, a layer of luminous mist covered everything. Fincayra's trees, rivers, canyons, and even its people, carried that vaporous sheen. *Cloudskin*, as people called it.

It was that unusual misty quality, together with Fincayra's celebrated history, that made this place such an exotic destination for travelers. Yet given the great difficulty of getting here—the route required mastery of several unpredictable portals (including one hidden deep inside an ocean of mist)—Fincayra was very seldom visited. Only the most seasoned explorers took the journey . . . and nobody fit that description better than Avalon's adventurous duo, Serella and Krystallus.

"Look here," said Krystallus with a shake of his white mane. "I thought we came all the way here for a pleasant day of climbing in Eagles' Canyon. Not for a fit of shouting."

"I'm not shouting!" yelled Serella. She frowned. "Just—er, well, *protesting*. Your absolute idiocy!"

"Look, I—"

"How could you ever give that map away?" She stamped her boot on the ledge, spraying shreds of glowing mist in all directions. "You might as well give away that stellar compass I gave you."

"Never!" he objected.

Stepping closer, Krystallus reached out his hand and touched the coil of sturdy elven rope that she wore slung over her shoulder. He ran a finger down the rope, as silky smooth as the stalks of purple ribbonflax from which it had been woven. Then, very gently, he continued to run his finger along the length of her arm.

In a much quieter voice, he said, "I'd never give that compass away, for any reason."

She raised an eyebrow, her face full of doubt.

"And not because of the marvelous things it can do," he continued. "Nor the fact that I'll need it someday to climb up to the stars." He peered at her. "No, I'd never give it away . . . because of who gave it to me."

She shook her arm, tossing his hand aside. "How am I supposed to believe that? If you gave away a magical map that can only be used once—there's no telling what you'll do next."

"You're not listening!" he growled, his voice rising again. "I did it to help Basil. In his fight."

"His fight?"

"Yes, Serella. I told you already! He needs the map. To try to save . . ." He paused to clear his throat. "Everything he's been fighting for all these years."

"Which is what?" She scowled at him so fiercely that the pointed tips of her ears turned crimson. "What exactly is so precious, so important, that it was worth giving away your map?"

"Avalon! All those places that Basil and my fa—, er, Merlin—care so much about. Love so dearly."

Serella's face softened. Cupping her hand, she slid it across the canyon wall, filling her palm with mist. The luminous vapors rested inside her hand like a small, glowing cloud.

"This mist," she said gently, "belongs to Fincayra. It covers these cliffs the way it covers everything else around here. But even if we can't see the cliffs, they are still there."

He furrowed his brow. "What are you getting at?"

"Sometimes," she went on, looking at the small cloud within her hand, "people are like that. All we notice is what's on the surface—the pain, the mist that covers our deeper feelings. Not the feelings themselves, the hard rock beneath."

Krystallus swallowed. "You're saying . . . this isn't really about the map?"

"Right."

"And it isn't really about Avalon?"

"Right . . . at least, that's not the most important part."

Krystallus, bewildered, ran a hand over his forehead and through his long white hair. "Then what *is* all this about? If not the map, or Avalon, what else could it be? I don't have a clue."

Her eyes, forest green, peered at him. "Go deeper. To the hard rock beneath."

"Maybe . . . ," he began, then caught himself. "No, that's not it."

Serella's eyebrows lifted, but she didn't speak.

He scuffed his boot along the ledge, plowing through the layer of mist. Hesitantly, he asked, "You don't think this is about Merlin? My relationship with him?"

She merely gazed at him.

"But that's absurd!"

The gaze didn't waver.

"Really, Serella. That's ridiculous. Impossible."

His brow creased. "How . . . could this possibly have anything to do with Merlin?"

She cocked her head to one side, making her silvery blond hair spill over one shoulder. "He is your father, you know."

"Even if he never acted like one," grumbled Krystallus. "Why, even when I was little, he made it clear that I . . ."

"Go on."

"That I wasn't as important to him as all his special places! His special world!"

The elf maiden nodded. "Avalon."

"Yes, Avalon." He clenched his jaw. "He treated me as badly as . . . well, as . . . his father treated *him*. Made me feel he loved his world, Avalon, a whole lot more than . . ."

"His own son."

Surprised by the power of her words, he drew a sharp breath. Blinking his eyes, he muttered, "Cursed mist! Fogging my vision."

"Right," she said softly. "Mist can do that."

He stared at her. "I'm a grown man, Serella! Explorer. Founder of a college for mapmakers. You really believe it still hurts me that Merlin loved those places so much? And you really believe that's why I gave the map away?"

"Not why you gave it away." She blew slowly on the cloud in her palm, making it melt into the air. "But why you can't bring yourself to admit that you gave it away to help *Avalon*. The world you love every bit as much as Basil does. And every bit as much as your father does."

Krystallus scowled. "That's absurd! Far-fetched. Idiotic." He squeezed his fists, then slowly relaxed them. "And . . . absolutely right."

Serella leaned closer and kissed him tenderly on the lips. "That's what I love about you. You may be a slow learner . . . but at least you're honest."

His eyes narrowed. "And you know what I love about you?"

"What?"

"That you're so easy to beat in a climb!" He gave her rope a tug. "Come on. I'll race you to that next ledge up there."

Before he'd even finished talking, Serella had turned to the cliff wall and found her first handhold. Krystallus grinned, then did the same, grasping the rock that lay beneath the mist.

15: AN INSTINCT

I would wager a mountain of dragons' scales that rash boldness
will always appeal more than wisdom. And if you somehow
survive the boldness, you might become a bit wiser.

Like a pair of oversized spiders, Krystallus and Serella
climbed the cliff wall. A constant cascade of mist poured
over them as they worked their way higher, washing over their
heads and backs, soaking their tunics and leggings. As they
raced up to the next ledge, their hands and feet barely touched
a hold before reaching for the next one.

After several minutes of uninterrupted climbing, neither
one of them had pulled ahead. And neither showed any sign
of slowing down. Meanwhile, both climbers continued to
pant hard, drip with sweat and mist, and strain every muscle
from their fingertips down to their toes.

An eagle glided past, nearly brushing Serella's back with
an outstretched wing tip. The bird's mighty screech echoed
across the cliffs. Yet even that explosion of sound didn't break
the racers' concentration. Without a second's pause, they kept
on climbing.

For years, they had raced each other, challenging themselves to go higher or faster or deeper, in many varied places. Whether they climbed the misty cliffs of Fincayra, swam between the islands of the Rainbow Seas, dived for luminous fish in the Swaying Sea, or hiked to the summits of Stoneroot's high peaks, they always raced. Not merely to win, but to enjoy the exhilarating sense of pushing themselves to their limits.

At last they neared the ledge. Krystallus jammed the toe of his boot into a notch, transferred his weight to that foot— then heard a loud *craaack*. Suddenly the notch broke off, sending shards of rock bouncing down the cliff into the canyon far below.

Krystallus cried out in surprise. He leaped aside and groped desperately for a new hold. Just as he started to slip—

Found it! His fingers plunged into a narrow seam, sturdy enough to hold his weight so that he wouldn't join the shower of shards. While his elven rope, secured to the cliff face, would have kept him from tumbling all the way down to the canyon floor, it couldn't have kept him from being badly injured. Or, even worse in his mind, from losing this race to Serella.

Hearing his cry, the elf maiden did something she hadn't done since their race began. She paused. Not for long, just for a heartbeat—enough time to be sure that her favorite climbing partner was not going to fall to his death. But that brief pause was enough to give Krystallus the edge.

He continued to climb, never hesitating. By the time Serella resumed, he was already a few hands' lengths ahead. Though they moved upward at an identical pace, finding new holds beneath the layer of mist, he maintained his slight lead.

Krystallus's fingers grasped the lip of the ledge. He pulled himself up, despite the quaking muscles of his arms and shoulders. With a groan that mixed exhaustion and pride, he lay flat on his back, both his legs still dangling over the edge. As thoroughly tired as he was, he still had enough strength to grin.

Right after that, Serella hoisted herself onto the rocky ledge. Like him, she collapsed onto her back; like him, she panted ceaselessly. But unlike Krystallus, she didn't grin.

Instead, she wore a full-blown smile.

"Not fair!" she exclaimed through heaving breaths. "I think . . . you staged . . . that whole thing. Just . . . to slow me down."

"Think so?" He raised himself up on one elbow and gazed at her. Panting heavily, he asked, "Isn't that why . . . you kissed me . . . back at the start? A trick . . . to wreck . . . my concentration?"

Serella, too, propped herself up on an elbow. Green eyes glittering, she replied, "Smart man."

"Well, then, I guess . . . I owe you one."

She cocked her head, puzzled. "You mean . . . a trick?"

"No." He slid nearer on the ledge, sending a wave of mist across her body. "I mean this."

He leaned over and gave her a kiss, alive with passion.

"There," he announced, pulling away. "Now we're even."

"No." She shook her head, scattering the mist that had settled on her hair. "I think I won."

He grinned once more. "I'll try to do better next time."

"You're doing fine."

Abruptly, his joviality vanished. "Not really, Serella." He glanced at the eagle, now merely a distant silhouette gliding through the canyon, then turned back to her. "What you said to me back there—you were right. About . . . my father. And how much I love Avalon."

She sat up, pulling her knees toward her chest, all the while studying him. "You want to help somehow?"

He nodded, swishing his long mane against his shoulders. "It's too late, I fear, to help Basil. And too late to do anything with that map. But it's not too late—"

"To do something utterly crazy," she completed. "Am I right?"

"My specialty." Though he tried to sound lighthearted, he didn't succeed. "It's a long shot. But it could, perhaps, be useful."

"What are you thinking?"

Krystallus drew a deep breath of misty air. "I've been hearing, for some time now, about strange things happening in the Haunted Marsh."

"The Marsh?" Despite being a veteran explorer of treacherous places, Serella frowned. "That's the last place you should go if you want to do something helpful. It's just a wasteland— and a death trap."

Rubbing the stubble on his chin, Krystallus replied, "That . . . and maybe something more."

"Like what?" she asked with a scowl.

"Almost a year ago, one of my best young mapmakers, Vespwyn—"

"I met him," she interrupted. "He was with you that time we trekked to the birthplace of sylphs in Airroot."

"Right. Well, you remember, then, he had the heart of a true explorer."

"As much," she admitted, "as anyone who is not an elf."

Ignoring her jab, he continued, "Vespwyn told me that he'd passed near the borders of the Marsh several times in recent years, and he'd witnessed something disturbing. Not just the usual moaning and groaning of marsh ghouls—who aren't, in any case, as thoroughly bad as most people think. No, this was something worse, much worse."

"What?" asked Serella, her tone skeptical.

"He didn't say. The only words he used were 'dark—too dark' and 'trouble for Avalon.' He insisted on finding out more. And, over my objections, on going alone." Krystallus pinched his lips, then said, "He never came back."

"So you want to find out what happened to him. That's understandable. But he could have died a thousand different ways in that horrible place! What's the point of risking your life, too?"

"It's those words—*trouble for Avalon*. Vespwyn didn't say such a thing lightly. For him, protecting this world was the highest ideal anyone could live by. In that way, he was a lot like my father."

Serella blew a long breath. Softly, she said, "Just as you are."

He shrugged. "I suppose you're right. Although Merlin would never agree, that's certain! Nothing I can ever do will change his opinion of me. Nothing. But anyway, that doesn't matter."

Watching him, she raised an eyebrow.

He squared his shoulders. "All that matters is helping Avalon survive! And when I put together what Vespwyn said with the rumors I've heard for too long now, I need to investigate. It could be nothing. Or it could be important—a key to our world's troubles."

She brushed a spiraling curl of mist off her nose. "I can tell you need to do this."

"I need, at least, to try."

She nodded. "I only wish I could come with you. But I have to lead that expedition to High Brynchilla, you know, and the ships are sailing tomorrow."

"I know." Reaching out his hand, he took hers, weaving his fingers into her own. "You'll still be with me."

"How will you get there?" she probed. "That swamp is about as accessible as a fire dragon's throat."

"The portal in northern Malóch. Just inside the desert, near the place bards call Hidden Gate. I can trek from there."

"Too bad you don't have a magical map to guide you," she said teasingly.

"Right." Humor played across his lips. "Next time I do something rash, I'll check with you first."

"No, you won't."

Serella waved her hand through the vaporous air, sending a small gust of wind toward the cliff wall. Its layer of luminous mist rippled and parted, revealing the moist rock underneath. She watched the undulating mist, her face solemn, then turned back to Krystallus.

"And that," she added, "is another thing I love about you."

16: WINGS

Returning home can sometimes be the strangest journey of all.

Basilgarrad flew over the high peaks of Olanabram, his enormous wings stretching wider than the blue-tinted glaciers below. Much as he would have liked to fly even faster, the dragon held his glides between strokes as long as possible, riding on the whistling wind, so that he wouldn't outpace Marnya and Ganta. As it was, he could hear their labored breathing not far behind as they struggled to stay with him.

Below, his shadow floated over the glaciers, snowfields, and summits of the peaks. Basilgarrad watched the changing scene, noticing how his jagged wings seemed to twist, shorten, and expand as the shadow moved across the steepest slopes. Just as he reached Hallia's Peak, the summit where he'd parted with Merlin all those years ago, he felt a familiar tap on the edge of his ear.

"Good to be back here, old chap." The wizard's voice, spoken right into the huge, pointed ear that he was holding tightly, rang louder than the whistling wind. Merlin ran his hand affectionately over the long green hairs that lined the ear's edge, as if he were stroking a puppy. "We've seen quite a few adventures down there, haven't we?"

"We have," boomed Basilgarrad, nodding his massive head as he flew. "Starting with your wedding."

"Right! I'd almost forgotten you were there—seeing as how you came disguised as a puny little lizard with dried up leaves for wings."

The dragon's throat rumbled with laughter, sounding like an approaching thunderstorm. "The smallest package can sometimes hold the biggest surprise."

Merlin stroked the back of his friend's ear. "Indeed. You'd have said the same about me if you had known me as a bumbling young man."

"As compared to the bumbling old man you are now?"

"Look here, Basil. That sort of remark is, well . . ."

"At a loss for words, are we?" the dragon teased. "Or are you simply searching for one of your tangled strings of long-worded wizard's babble?"

"Babble? By the breath of Dagda, you insult me! If I ever use strings of long words, it's merely . . ."

"What?"

"A serendipitous concatenation of happenstance, that's what." For good measure, the wizard added, "Indubitably."

Basilgarrad's great head bobbed slightly. "I see."

Above them, the sky began to ripple with rays of golden light, the daily display of starset. As the stars of Avalon grew dimmer, bright hues painted the sky as well as the snowy lands below. Basilgarrad's shadow, like those of the two smaller dragons behind him, seemed to sail across a frozen sea whose waves glittered with gold.

"Basil," said Merlin, a new urgency in his voice, "I think it would be wise to stop somewhere for the night."

"Stop somewhere?" roared the green dragon. He swiveled his ears in surprise, nearly knocking Merlin off his perch. "We have no time to lose!"

The wizard yelped and clutched the hairs inside the dragon's ear, barely hanging on. Cursing quietly, he pulled himself upright. At last, he stood again—this time with both arms wrapped around the ear, his blue robe fluttering in the wind. Deep inside his beard, Euclid clacked his beak angrily, scolding him for being so clumsy.

"It wasn't my fault," grumbled Merlin. He reached a hand toward his beard, meaning to scratch the tufted feathers atop the owl's head—then suddenly realized he could get nipped and pulled his hand away. "Try to show some understanding, will you?"

In answer, the owl gave a savage snap of his beak.

Frowning, the wizard turned back to Basilgarrad's ear. "It's going to be night very soon," he explained. "The Marsh will be terribly dark. The worst possible time to attack." He chewed thoughtfully on a few strands of his beard. "I have a feeling we're going to need every bit of daylight we can find in that accursed place, just to keep our bearings. Let alone to fight that monster."

Basilgarrad's brow furrowed, bending the green scales under the wizard's feet. "But our time is short enough already! Something horrible is happening there, even now. I can feel it."

"So can I, old friend." Merlin tapped the back of the dragon's ear. "But waiting until dawn isn't going to change anything." Under his breath, he muttered, "I hope."

The dragon growled so fiercely that his whole neck and head vibrated, almost making Merlin lose his balance again. "All right, then. We'll land for the night. Somewhere close to the Haunted Marsh, but not so close we'll be discovered."

"I know just the place," replied Merlin. He leaned into the hollow of the ear, whispering his idea.

Before he had even finished, the dragon tilted his wings and angled downward. Close behind, Marnya and Ganta followed. Meanwhile, the night deepened. The world grew swiftly darker, broken only by the faint glitter of starlight on the dragons' wings. They seemed to be descending into another world, one made of steadily darkening shadows.

17: THE BLACK GASH

Where, I wonder, was Dagda on that night we needed him most?

Shifting the angle of his great wings, Basilgarrad descended rapidly. All around him, night deepened, cloaking the lands below in mysterious veils of gray and black, streaked now and then with shimmering silver from the stars. If he hadn't known where he was flying, he couldn't have been certain whether those dark veils covered mountains, forests, or seas.

He was in no mood, however, to appreciate the scenery. His voice rumbled as his powerful claws raked the air, clutching at nothing—signs of his overwhelming frustration. Why couldn't they simply plunge into the Haunted Marsh and attack that miserable beast of darkness right now? Before it could do its next terrible deed, whatever that might be?

Because that would be stupid, Basil. The wizard, who had heard the dragon's frustrated thoughts, shot back a blunt reply. *I really think—*

You think too much, came the equally blunt retort, cutting him off. *I agreed to wait until morning, but I didn't agree to like it.*

Merlin, his arms wrapped around the dragon's ear, sighed heavily. He glanced down at the silver stars that embroidered his robe's flowing sleeves. In the constant wind of flying, the sleeves flapped and fluttered, making the stars seem to shimmer—as if they were, themselves, connected to the quivering lights in Avalon's sky.

Basilgarrad glanced behind, checking on their winged companions. Despite the deepening gloom, he could see Marnya's blue scales glittering as she moved her flippers. Would he soon regret having taught that water dragon how to fly? Would this battle prove too much for even her adventurous spirit?

He frowned, scrunching the scales of his snout. Questions like that he couldn't begin to answer. The future remained hidden, as impossible to see as young Ganta, who was flying somewhere behind Marnya.

A flash of blue, brighter than her luminous scales, caught his attention. Marnya's eye! For an instant their gazes met, connecting them across that distance, while their eyes glowed in the darkness like a sapphire and an emerald.

Only because he sensed the nearness of land, Basilgarrad turned away. Just in time, too. A large, undulating shape loomed right below them. He tilted both wings backward to catch the air and slow himself for landing.

"There it is," said Merlin into the dragon's ear. "The great sand dune I told you about. We're only a few leagues from the Marsh, just a short hop over the desert. But behind this dune, we can wait for dawn in secret."

The dragon lifted his head and arched his back as he prepared to hit the ground. The trick wouldn't be landing safely, despite the dark of night. No, the difficulty would be landing quietly—setting down his enormous body without making noise that could alert their enemies.

Wind rushed across Basilgarrad's face, much warmer than before. All at once he thought of another warm wind, his wandering friend Aylah. Could it be her? He sniffed the air, searching for the wind sister's familiar scent of cinnamon.

Alas, he smelled only sand, sand, and more sand. He flared his nostrils and snorted in dismay. When would he finally forget about her? She had left Avalon forever, and told him so herself. Why couldn't he just believe that?

Slam! His massive chest struck the valley of sand beneath the dune. He skidded forward, grinding across the desert, pumping his wings backward to slow down. Sand sprayed in all directions, blocking out the stars and swirling like a storm.

He came, at last, to a stop. Sand rained down on his back and wings, plinking against his scales. Merlin, still clutching the dragon's ear, shook his head to shake the sand out of his beard. But he shook so hard that Euclid screeched and flew out of the tangled gray forest where he'd made his nest.

In the deep darkness, it was impossible to see where the owl flew. Thanks to the constant clacking of his little beak, though, it was easy to follow his flight with great precision. This was, Basilgarrad suddenly realized, a flight path unlike any he'd ever encountered.

Yes, Basil, offered Merlin upon hearing his companion's thoughts. *Euclid is indeed flying in geometric patterns! Why, there's his square—and there, a pentagram. Can't you hear him clack his beak at all the angles?* The wizard chuckled. *That's why he isn't clacking now. He's doing a circle.*

"But why?" asked the dragon aloud. "What's the purpose of flying"—he paused while the owl cut a sharp corner of an octagon, dangerously close to the dragon's eye—"like that?"

Merlin shrugged as he pulled his staff out of the loop in his belt. "Who knows? You might as well ask the original Euclid, a bright young fellow I met in Greece—an intriguing place, if you like wearing baggy robes and laurel wreaths all the time—just why he spent so much time drawing shapes. It's impossible to tell."

An abrupt grinding noise kept Basilgarrad from responding. A new spray of sand filled the air as Marnya landed, skidding to a halt beside the green dragon. He lifted his right wing so she wouldn't slide into it, then lightly draped it across her back. With the tip of his wing, he gently tapped the smooth scales on her shoulder.

Just then, with a flutter of small wings, Ganta, too, landed. Yet he chose to touch down not on the sand, but on the tip of Basilgarrad's snout.

"I'm here, master Basil," the little fellow proudly announced. He took several gulps of air, then added, "Right here with you."

"So I see." The great dragon lifted the corner of his mouth

in a slight grin, since Ganta's pluckiness reminded him of his own when he, too, had been small.

"When do we fly into battle?" Ganta asked, eagerly tapping his tiny claws on the scale beneath him.

"At dawn," rumbled his uncle, not happily. He snorted for emphasis, blowing a gust of sand.

Euclid screeched at the sound. He instantly cut short a parallelogram and flew, instead, back to Merlin's beard. With one final clack of his beak, the little owl plunged again into the tangle of hairs, burrowing inside.

"Dawn will come soon," promised the wizard, his voice grim. "In some ways, too soon."

"What do you mean by that?" demanded the dragon.

"I feel we're flying blind—and not just because it's nighttime. Mainly I wish we knew more about this monster— especially where its power comes from."

"How would that help?" asked Marnya, shifting anxiously under Basilgarrad's wing.

"If we understood the source of its power, we might know better how to fight it." He twirled a strand of his beard— down at the bottom, well out of reach of Euclid's beak. "As it is, we know almost nothing."

"We know it serves Rhita Gawr," offered Marnya. "Maybe all its power comes from its master in the spirit realm."

"Originally, yes." The wizard shook his head glumly. "But once it arrived here in Avalon, it must have found another source. Fortunately for all of us, there is no direct link between Avalon and the Otherworld of the Spirits. If there were," he said in an ominous tone, "its power would be . . . unthinkable."

"And unstoppable." Marnya glanced at her chosen mate. "Even the incredible strength of Basilgarrad would be no match for an immortal like Rhita Gawr."

"Don't be so sure," he rumbled, flexing his mighty tail to lift the deadly knob into the air.

Ganta pranced across the dragon's nose. "That's the spirit!"

"Not if we want to survive tomorrow," countered Merlin. He started to pace on the sand at the base of the dune. "We need more than courage to win this battle, I'm afraid."

Basilgarrad lowered his massive head to the sand. Without thinking about it, he used his magic to produce the sweet, lingering smell of lilac blossoms, a smell from his youth in the fragrant forest of Woodroot. Something about that smell never failed to cheer him whenever he felt despondent.

Marnya jolted to attention, her head erect. She sniffed the air several times. "What is that smell?"

"It's your talented friend there," explained Merlin. "Among Basil's many skills is—"

"This totally useless one," finished the dragon himself. He cocked an ear toward the wizard. "He casts spells, I cast smells. One can change the world; the other . . . a breeze. Not fair, is it?"

Marnya raised her flipper and, with its webbing, touched his great brow. Stroking his scales, she said quietly, "Not every power is measured by brute strength, my dearest. Sometimes, one little smell can lift a mood—and that, in its own way, could change the world."

Gratitude shone in Basilgarrad's eyes. While he said nothing, it didn't surprise Marnya that, an instant later, the smell of lilacs suddenly vanished. In its place wafted a new aroma—the unmistakably briny smell of the sea.

"The ocean," she said with a dreamy sigh.

"Not just any ocean," the green dragon remarked. "Can you smell the hints of iridescent algae and gillywoggle kelp? That, Marnya, is found in only one place. True?"

She nodded, making the scales of her nose glisten with starlight. "The Rainbow Seas. My home."

In the dim glow of the stars above, they looked at each other for a long moment. It didn't occur to either of them how odd it was to be smelling the salty scent of those colorful waters here, in a faraway desert where any rainbow would be overwhelmed by the gloom of night. All that mattered was that, for this moment at least, they were together.

Merlin stopped pacing. His voice wistful, he said, "Once, long ago it seems . . . I looked at someone that way." He swallowed. "And I lost her too soon."

Marnya turned her sleek, blue-tinted face toward him. "Hallia," she said gently. "Did you know that she is revered in dragon lore? As the only person of her kind who ever raised a dragon from infancy?"

"My mother!" piped Ganta excitedly. He slapped Basilgarrad's snout with his little tail. "You're talking about her."

"That's right," answered Merlin. "She raised your mother,

Gwynnia, with all the great care she gave to our own son, Krys—" He caught himself, and pinched his lips. "To someone else she loved."

Basilgarrad's long neck trembled as he released a deep growl. "He is still your son. In more ways than you know—or will admit."

Though Merlin's downturned face was too dark to see, the dragon had no doubt that his old friend was frowning. "Perhaps," suggested Basilgarrad, "the time has come for you two to meet again. A fresh start. A new future."

Merlin slowly raised his head. "Perhaps. But I doubt he would ever allow that to happen. Not after . . ."

His words trailed off, merging with the sound of the desert wind that whisked across the sand dune. "Besides, Basil, you know as well as I do that *none of us* will have a new future unless we can somehow defeat that monster in the Marsh."

Deep wrinkles formed on the wizard's brow, covering his forehead and disappearing under the wild white hair that protruded from under the rim of his hat. "And instead of the hope and confidence I'd like to feel right now, all I feel is . . . doubt. Deep, painful doubt."

"Wait!" thundered Basilgarrad. He lifted his enormous head off the sand. "That could be the answer."

"To what?" asked Merlin and Marnya simultaneously.

"To your question about the source of its power." The dragon's eyes glowed so bright they seemed ablaze. "It began as a leech, remember? A disgusting little beast who lived by sucking other creatures' blood. Then it grew much bigger, stronger—and also darker—by sucking something else. Some other kind of nourishment."

Puzzled, Merlin tilted his head. "I don't follow you."

The dragon brought his face closer, so that his immense lower lip almost touched Merlin. "What if, instead of blood, it found some way to drink pain and sorrow? What if its strength comes from suffering? From any sort of negative energy?"

Merlin's back straightened. In the green glow of the dragon's eyes, he nodded. "So all these years of brutal fighting in Avalon—the entire War of Storms—was more than just a distraction. More than just a way to keep you so busy you wouldn't find its hiding place."

"Yes! All that horror—the greed, arrogance, hatred, and killing—was also its food. Its source of power." Basilgarrad's voice lowered to its deepest level. "That beast has grown stronger in direct proportion to Avalon's misery."

Marnya shuddered. "How horrible! So even my father's death gave it more power."

As Basilgarrad touched her flipper with his wing tip, a gust of wind blew over them, pelting their bodies with sand. One lone grain struck the green dragon's lip, bounced between his rows of terrible teeth, and struck the tip of his tongue. He started, swiveling his ears. For the unexpected touch of that tiny object reminded him of Dagda's command, long ago, that he must swallow a single grain of sand from every realm. While he had finally succeeded, taking a small taste of all Avalon's realms, he never understood why. No matter how many years had passed, nor how many leagues he had flown, Dagda's purpose remained as mysterious as ever.

He looked up into the starry sky, wondering where Dagda might be now. And why, through Avalon's long years of agony, the great spirit had never come in person to stop all the madness, all the misery. Sure, he'd sent down the vision of a great stag who commanded the dragon to swallow those grains of sand. Yet that stag was only a small fragment of the real god Dagda, powerful leader of the spirit realm. Why hadn't he just *intervened*, in the same way Rhita Gawr had long tried to do? Although, of course, their goals couldn't be more different: Rhita Gawr wanted to invade and conquer this world, not save it from suffering.

You answered your own question, Basil. Merlin reached up and touched the dragon's lower lip with the top of his staff. "Dagda," he said aloud, "values our free will, our power of choice—something that Rhita Gawr completely disregards. To Dagda, we are mortals with the right to choose our own destiny; to Rhita Gawr, we are merely obstacles in his path."

"Still," grumbled the dragon, "we certainly could use his help right now."

"That we could," agreed Merlin. Raising his bushy eyebrows, he studied the constellations overhead. His gaze roamed from Pegasus to the Twisted Tree to the spot where the seven stars of the Wizard's Staff once blazed. Peering at that empty place, he frowned. And then gasped.

"Basil, look!" he cried, pointing his staff at the black gash in the sky.

Basilgarrad and Marnya both stared at the spot. So did little Ganta, perched on his uncle's snout. Like the wizard, they gasped in horror.

For all of them could see, stretching down from the center of the vanished constellation, a thin, writhing line of utter darkness. Like a monstrous serpent, it reached downward, groping for its goal.

Avalon.

"Quick!" shouted Merlin. "We must go to the Haunted Marsh."

"But it's not yet dawn," objected Marnya. "You said—"

"Forget what I said! If we don't go now, there may never *be* another dawn."

"Right," agreed Basilgarrad. He slammed his huge tail on the sand, heedless of the explosion of grains all around. "It's time to fly."

18: HIDDEN GATE

All it takes to see a new world is to look more closely at the old one.

The afternoon before Basilgarrad and his companions landed at the sand dune, someone else arrived at the same desert. Just five leagues to the east, a lone figure stepped out of a flaming portal at the desert's edge. Green fire crackled all around him, grasping at his tunic, leggings, and boots. But he strode out of the flames without even a sideways glance, for he'd passed through many portals before.

Krystallus's boots crunched on the sand. That gritty sound alone would have been enough to assure him that he had arrived at his intended destination. And the vista before him was even more convincing. Nearly all he could see, as his explorer's eyes scanned the horizon, was desert—dunes of sand, vales of sand, and swirling storms of sand. But for the slight variations in color from golden brown to rusty red, it all looked the same.

He spotted only two exceptions. Pivoting slightly, he gazed at the first, a majestic spire of rust-colored rock that seemed to glow in the late afternoon light. Carved over the centuries by windblown sand, the spire rose upward like a solid column—until, more than fifty man-heights above the desert, it opened into an enormous circle. This great, rough-hewn circle seemed to be a passageway to some distant world, or a different kind of portal that led to the clouds and sky beyond. Legends told of a band of elves from the forest of Africqua who had left their homes and families to try to climb through the opening—and never came back.

"No wonder," Krystallus said aloud as he peered in wonder at the tower, "you are called the Hidden Gate."

At that moment, a long-necked cormorant flew steadily toward the spire. As the bird drew nearer, it seemed to be aiming straight at the circle. With every beat of its black wings, it came closer, until Krystallus felt certain the bird was going to try to fly through the opening. He stood rigid, watching carefully, his boots so fixed to the sand that he resembled a spire himself.

As the bird approached, it stretched its neck out to full length. This bird, thought Krystallus, just can't wait to pass through the hole! He grinned. *A fellow explorer.*

He noticed, just then, how the afternoon light played across the rocky surface. *That's strange*, he told himself. The shifting light made the stone appear to move. The circle's edges actually seemed to flow inward, rippling like a rust-colored stream.

A split second before the cormorant reached the glowing circle, it screeched in surprise. But it didn't turn away. With another wingbeat, it plunged into the circle and—

Disappeared. Krystallus caught his breath. *It's gone. To-tally gone!*

He shook his head in disbelief, making his white mane dance across his shoulders. Never taking his eyes off the mysterious spire, he reached into his tunic pocket and pulled out his sketchbook. With practiced motions, he also retrieved his vial of octopus ink, removed the cork, and dipped his feather pen into the black liquid.

Looking away for the first time, he opened the sketchbook to a blank page. Scrawling the words *Hidden Gate, Malóch,* on the bottom of the page, he hastily drew the spire—complete with the black cormorant about to enter the circle. Using his lightest touch, he penned some rippling lines around the stone's edges, lines meant to evoke light or magic . . . or both.

He held the book before his face, glancing back and forth at the tower to check for accuracy. Carefully, he added a few more lines and shadows for texture. Satisfied at last, he closed the sketchbook with a *snap*. Then he replaced it, along with the feather and ink vial, in his pocket.

"Someday," he said to the spire, "I will come back here. And explore your mysteries." He gave a firm nod. "That's a promise."

He peered at the strange opening for a few more seconds. "Right now, though, I have another place to go."

Slowly, he turned to the north, to face the only other thing he could see that was not sand. It was impossible to miss. On the horizon, rising into the sky, billowed a group of thick, black clouds. Yet, unlike any storm clouds he'd ever seen, these seemed so dark they were not made of vapors— nor any physical substance. No, these clouds seemed to be made from the *absence* of anything else. Including light.

Krystallus chewed his lip thoughtfully. *The Haunted Marsh. Whatever is happening there, it can't be good.* He swallowed, knowing that whatever it was, he would soon find out.

Squinting, he estimated the distances. *Four leagues, maybe five. I should be there before starset.*

He reached into another breast pocket. This time he pulled out a glass globe bound with a leather strap, the remarkable compass Serella had given him. Tilting the globe in his hands, he watched its twin silver arrows, suspended by hair-thin wires, spin around in a magical dance. One of those arrows, he knew, always pointed starward—to the uttermost heights of the Great Tree. But today he kept his attention on the other arrow, which guided him in travels across the root-realms of Avalon.

"Fifty-seven degrees," he observed, checking the bearing for the Haunted Marsh. Although his destination was easily visible, he knew from experience that he couldn't be sure this visibility would last. His view of the Marsh could be obscured by a sandstorm or altered by some sort of mirage. If something like that happened, he could now set a bearing and find his way.

Giving silent thanks to Serella, he returned the compass to his tunic. He took a deep breath of desert air, then pulled a leather flask from his belt and took a few swallows of water. Finally, he started walking toward the looming mass of darkness.

"I'm not looking forward to this," he muttered as he took his first steps across the expanse of sand. The Haunted Marsh, and whatever deadly secrets it held, was of course foremost on his mind. But there was something else about this journey that troubled him almost as much, something he wished he could avoid.

The desert. Of all the varied places he'd encountered in a life of exploration—oceans, forests, deep caves, islands, air-scapes, high peaks, swamps, firelands, and more—he liked deserts the least. The few he'd seen were hot, dry, and devoid of life. While he'd never spent much time in deserts (today would be his longest trek through one), he felt no desire to change that fact.

He strode along, his boots grinding the sand with every step. Casually, he noted an undulating line of sand, no higher than his toe, that ran across his direction of travel. Like a miniature wall, it snaked across the desert. For no particular reason, he stopped walking and kicked a gap in the wall. Then, to see what might happen, he placed one foot into the gap. Within seconds, the gentle wind started to blow grains of sand across the toe of his boot, reconnecting the line that he had divided.

That little wall, he realized, *is rebuilding*.

Intrigued, he bent down on one knee to watch. Slowly, grain by grain, the wind piled sand on top of his boot, until the severed line was fully reconnected. Then, as if its work was done, the wind ceased raising the wall and merely blew along its length, moving sand horizontally instead of vertically. As long as the wall stood unbroken, the wind seemed perfectly content to flow along beside it, like a river beside its bank.

For the first time, he looked more closely at the desert floor. All around him, he suddenly saw, were more miniature walls. And all of them ran parallel to the one he had broken. Most of them stretched farther than he could see. Worked constantly by the wind, these parallel lines covered the entire surface.

Like waves! These little walls are like ocean waves. He cocked his head, surprised to find anything similar to the vast ocean in this equally vast desert. Maybe, he wondered, this is another kind of ocean—one made of sand.

Lifting his face to the horizon, he saw a long line of dunes that formed another, much taller kind of undulating wall. One dune in particular caught his attention, for it rose much higher than the rest. Could those dunes, he puzzled, also have been formed by the desert wind? Were they really giant waves?

He stood again. Brushing the sand off his knee, he noticed something else. A crusty bit of vegetation, as rusty red as the sand, had stuck to his legging. Some sort of leaf! He pulled it free and squeezed it between his thumb and finger, listening to its delicate crinkling sound. Then, looking down, he saw the rest of the small, leafy plant that his knee had crushed. A sturdy, flat-growing vine whose color matched the sand, it blended perfectly with its surroundings.

Impressed that anything could be so hardy as to grow here, Krystallus nodded in approval. *You are one tough little plant*, he thought. Curious, he lifted the red leaf to his tongue, just to see how it would taste.

"Bleccchhh!" He spat it out. *That's even worse than the deer lichen my mother fed me as a child.*

He spat out the bitter residue, then wiped his mouth on the sleeve of his tunic. Maybe, he realized, that vine's foul taste had helped it survive. And while he'd never be tempted to eat another bite, he had to admit the plant had earned his respect.

He was just about to start walking again when he happened to glance down at the place where he had spat. To his astonishment, the sand seemed to be moving, boiling with activity. Looking closer, he saw the source of all the commotion.

Monkeys! Tiny golden monkeys, each one smaller than his thumbnail, hopped around the moistened sand. They climbed over each other's backs, tugged on tails, and rolled across the ground as they drank and splashed in the remaining drops of liquid. To them, a lake had suddenly appeared in the desert— ample cause for celebration.

Amazed, Krystallus ran a hand through his hair. Miniature monkeys—what next? Cupping his ear, he could hear the faint squealing and chattering of these playful little creatures. Where had they been hiding? What did they do for water most of their lives? How many other creatures lived in this desert, unseen and undiscovered?

He grabbed his flask. Bending lower, he poured several

drops of water on the spot where the monkeys were playing. Shrieking with joy, they tumbled over each other, splashed wildly, and drank avidly from this marvelous new part of their landscape.

Krystallus gave them a few more drops, then stood. Gazing around him, he thought about how much more rich this place was than he'd first assumed. The desert held mountains, forests, and oceans of its own—full of variety, subtlety, and surprising discoveries. He had seen a magical gateway to places he couldn't fathom. Waves both very small and very large. An enormous dune. A hardy plant, so well disguised it looked like sand—and, for that matter, tasted like sand. A mass of tiny monkeys whose exuberant play lifted his spirits.

And I've walked only a few steps.

Turning back to the darkness billowing on the horizon, he resumed his trek. His senses felt fully reawakened. He scanned the surrounding sands, listened to the rustling wind, and sniffed the air for any strange scents. While he still felt the pang of foreboding about this journey, he also felt something more familiar—the thrill of exploration.

19: DISCOVERIES

Why is it that what we do know can save us, but what we don't know can kill us?

Hours later, Krystallus approached the Haunted Marsh. The golden flash of starset illuminated the sky, sending radiant ribbons across the heavens and signaling the start of night. But he hardly noticed, for his mind was teeming with thoughts of what he'd seen on his journey across the desert.

He paused to lean against an old elm tree that had, somehow, managed to take root in a cluster of rocks under a small dune. Beneath the elm's twisted branches, now tinted gold by the sky above, he sat down. After wedging himself between two gnarled roots, he pulled out his flask and gratefully took a swallow of water. Then he opened his sketchbook.

On a page that glowed with the golden light of starset, he reviewed his long list of discoveries from that day. He'd seen crowned lizards in five different colors, a giant desert snake (which was, fortunately, slithering up a distant dune), a radiant red butterfly, a three-horned ibex which leaped right over his head, and a family of sand-eating gnomes—in all, twenty-seven new kinds of creatures. And that did not count the luminous whirl of sand that had spun right up to him, stopped as if it were examining him closely, then twirled off in the opposite direction. It could have been a strangely condensed sandstorm, glowing from reflected light . . . or it could have been something else.

He drew a quick sketch of the mysterious whirl of sand, then closed the book. After giving its cover a satisfied tap, he replaced it in his tunic pocket. *What a day*, he told himself. *My first trek through this desert. But not my last.*

Looking over his shoulder, he could see, through the branches of the elm, the dense cloud that hovered over the land just half a league away. It billowed and churned, rising high into the sky. The Haunted Marsh. That cloud looked even darker than it had when he began this journey—a bottomless well of blackness.

He scrutinized the cloud. Within its dark, billowing folds, he spied a brief red glow that seemed to reveal a towering form, denser than the surrounding vapors. Maybe it was just the shifting light from starset, now rapidly fading. Or maybe not. *Whatever is hiding in there,* he vowed, *I will find it. And if it's linked to Avalon's troubles, I'll get the word to Basil.*

As night deepened, the cloud over the Marsh melted into the surrounding darkness. Krystallus watched, scowling. He knew better than to try to go into that swamp now. No, he'd stay safely camped under this ancient tree until dawn. Then, aided by the return of daylight, he would brave the Marsh.

In the quivering light of the stars, he studied the tree itself. Its knobby branches, once strong and sturdy, seemed to be sagging from age. Or was it from another, more sinister force? Clearly, where hundreds of healthy leaves once budded, only a few frail ones sprouted now. He rapped his knuckles on the root beside him. The wood felt hollow and distressed, making an echo that seemed to moan the words *baaaaack, go baaaaack*.

Krystallus placed his open hand on the tree's trunk. Beneath the flaking strips of bark, deep gouges ran through the column, cutting all the way into the heartwood. And yet, despite everything—poor soil, lack of water, nearness to the Marsh—this tree had somehow survived.

"You picked a terrible place to grow," he said, drumming his fingers against the old elm's trunk. "But here you are, even now. Still alive."

He nodded, part in admiration, part in sympathy. For he, too, knew something about growing up in difficult conditions—with an absent father whose love seemed always out of reach, with expectations for his own magic that he could never meet, and with the parched soil of a lonely life of aimless wandering. Until he'd met Serella.

Again he turned toward the Marsh. Now that the curtain of night had fallen, he could see almost no sign of the swamp. Almost. For unlike the desert dunes and plains surrounding him, no stars glittered above that place. No light at all penetrated the ominous cloud. Only the absence of light revealed the Marsh's existence.

Of course, he noticed other signs, as well. That faintly bitter smell on the desert wind—a smell that carried hints of

rotting plants, stale peat, and decayed flesh. And also that occasional whisper of sound, a warbling cry of anguish or a
distant scream.

One of those sounds pierced the night, a bone-chilling
shriek that seemed both far away and perilously close. Krystallus listened intently, scratching the stubble on his chin. That
was, he felt sure, the aching cry of a marsh ghoul. Travelers—
including the most worldly bards he knew, as well as the
seasoned explorers who visited Eopia College of Mapmakers—
considered marsh ghouls the most terrifying and irredeem-
ably evil beings in Avalon.

Krystallus, however, didn't agree. He knew better than to
assume they were hopelessly evil . . . especially after he'd discovered the secret tale of their origins. For just a few months
ago, he had found something precious. Something rich with
information. Something he'd been searching for throughout
his life.

Reaching into a tunic pocket, he removed a tattered,
leather-bound book, so old that wrinkles creased its cover like
the face of an elder friend. Gently, he ran his finger along the
binding. Then, with one finger, he tapped the leather clasp
that held the book closed, a clasp that wouldn't open with any
amount of force. Not even a mighty giant could have pulled
it apart.

No, as Krystallus knew, the clasp would open only with
the utterance of a secret password. After weeks of trial and
error, and much frustration, he'd been lucky enough to guess
the password. And he'd also been lucky in another respect:

The password didn't require any magic from whoever uttered it. All the necessary magic had been stored within the clasp by its maker—Merlin himself.

For this was Merlin's lost journal, hidden away by the wizard in the final days of his youth in Fincayra. It had lain for centuries in the mist-shrouded trunk of an ancient oak tree—a tree that Krystallus suspected was, in fact, none other than the famous Arbassa. It had taken many years of searching to find the tree, and then, almost coincidentally, to find the old book, but at last he'd succeeded.

Krystallus drew a slow breath, then said quietly, "Olo Eopia."

Hearing the password—Merlin's true name, given to him by Dagda before Fincayra merged with the spirit realm—the clasp suddenly stiffened as if it had come to life. All at once, its leather laces untied themselves and the small metal buckle in its center clicked. The clasp fell open.

Krystallus smiled. It felt good, for once, to feel as if he could work a little bit of magic. But his smile quickly faded. He knew that the feeling was only an illusion.

Unlike my father, he mused, *I don't have a single shred of magic—something he never understood. Sure, I can use magical objects like this book or an enchanted map—but any fool can do that. There is no magic inside me.* Merlin, he felt sure, never even thought about how much that fact had affected his son's life. Or how difficult it had made growing up in the shadow of a great wizard. *He never even wondered how hard it must be to have no magic of my own.*

Even so, discovering the lost journal had given Krystallus a new perspective on his father. In reading the wizard's own descriptions of events—many of which had become famous in folklore, stories he'd heard too many times to count—Krystallus realized that his father was, in fact, more than just a powerful figure of mythic proportions. He was also, at least in his youth, a passionate and impulsive person who could be unsure of himself, vulnerable, and even deathly afraid. He was, in sum, not just a wizard but also a human being.

Not so different, thought Krystallus, *from me.*

He opened the book, hearing the faint *crackle* of its binding. The pages, golden-edged and tattered from age, seemed to glow in the trembling light from the stars above. And also, it seemed, from a vague luminosity of their own.

He lifted the open book to his nose and inhaled. Its smell, something like a mixture of worn leather, parchment, and fire coals, filled his nostrils. The aroma, by now familiar, seemed to welcome him.

Lowering the book, he started to flip through its pages, looking for the passage about the marsh ghouls. He realized, with every turn of a page, that this volume was about much more than Merlin. It was, in truth, a treasure trove of stories, dreams, and histories of all sorts of people and places. Many of those stories had never been told before. Other than Serella and the young elf Tressimir, with whom he'd shared the journal, no one but Krystallus knew what marvels those pages contained.

Just before he came to the strange tale of the marsh

ghouls, his gaze fell upon a page that had been folded against itself. Carefully, he opened the page, finding a passage that he'd never read before. In Merlin's messy scrawl, more like the tracks of birds on a beach than penmanship meant to be legible, were these words:

In the days since I fought the magic-eating kreelix, a fight I only barely survived, I have wondered why I was cursed to be born a creature of magic. What do all these powers accomplish, except to make me a target for evil forces who want to kill or enslave me? Why must the people I love most, my mother and sister and beloved Hallia, suffer so much because of my affliction? How I wish I didn't have any magic of my own!

Stunned, Krystallus blinked his eyes. Had he read correctly? Had his father, in his stormy youth, really called his magic a curse and an affliction? Refocusing on the passage, he read on:

I can only hope that fate has given me these magical powers for a reason. A reason I must discover for myself. Somehow, I need to perceive my magic not as a burden—but as a gift. Something I can use to help the people and places I love. If only I felt confident of measuring up to such an enormous task!

Never mind such doubts. If this is my challenge, I accept it. And I also realize that it is equally difficult, in very different ways, for creatures who are born without any magic. Worst of all, I think, would be the fate of a nonmagical child whose father or mother possesses great powers. The very idea of such a child makes my heart ache, and reminds me how fortunate I truly am.

Krystallus blinked again, clearing his vision enough to

read that line again: *The very idea of such a child makes my heart ache.*

He shifted his weight, leaning back against the old elm. As he did so, the journal's magical clasp brushed against his thumb. All at once, he realized something new about the clasp. About the journal. And about his father.

What if Krystallus hadn't merely been lucky that the password required no magic beyond what already resided in the clasp? What if Merlin had planned it that way—so that even a person with no magic of his own could someday read this secret journal?

He swallowed. What if . . . Merlin had only wanted the journal to be read by someone who knew the wizard well enough to know his true name—Olo Eopia? Someone who could be his own child, a son or daughter yet to be born.

Me, thought Krystallus. *He wanted this journal to come to me.*

In the distance, a shrieking wail arose. Krystallus recognized the sound at once. With a final glance at the passage he'd just discovered, he turned to the section on the marsh ghouls. He'd read the description of their tragic history many times before, but never with so much interest as now.

Long ago in Lost Fincayra, on wondrous meadows filled with flowers, lived a community of enchantresses, the Xania-Soe. They lived peacefully, amassing their wealth not in jewels or weapons but in knowledge. So great was their wisdom, it was said, the wind itself refused to blow over their realm, to avoid spreading dangerous knowledge to others. They learned how to bend time in a magical Mirror, as well as how to coax magical perfumes from the flowers. In time, the very air of that place smelled of magic. Powerful magic.

So powerful that the warlord Rhita Gawr tried to conquer that realm. And nearly succeeded. Unable to stop his invasion, the enchantresses decided to make a terrible sacrifice. Just before Rhita Gawr took control, they threw a curse on their beloved homeland—a curse that made their magical flowers spew poisons and curses into the air. Because no wind blew there, the poisons seeped into the land itself, turning life into death, light into shadow. The enchantresses refused to leave their cherished home, even in its bitter transformation. So they, too, were poisoned. Twisted by rage and grief, they became deadly, ghoulish beings—the marsh ghouls.

Krystallus tapped on the root beside him, thinking about their plight. He knew that those creatures—once so beautiful and admired, now so ghastly and feared—had migrated to Avalon, settling in the place known today as the Haunted Marsh. Feeling only wrath and sorrow, they had continued to bring revenge on anyone who dared to come near them. Only one person in history had ever faced the marsh ghouls and survived.

My father. Krystallus pursed his lips, wondering about exactly what had happened. The marsh ghouls, somehow, chose not only to spare Merlin, but to help him—most likely the only act of kindness they had ever performed. But why? The journal's description was sketchy; the only certainty was that their encounter had involved the magical Mirror.

Maybe someday, mused Krystallus, *I'll ask him to tell me.*

He bit his lip. *Or maybe not.* After the way he'd spoken to his father the last time they had met, Merlin would never want to see him again—let alone tell him the secrets of his lost years.

Deep in thought, he leaned back against the old elm's trunk. He didn't notice the sharp edges of the flaky bark that poked into his back. He didn't notice the rising chorus of chants that arose from the Marsh, pounding like distant drums. And he didn't notice the dark, ghoulish figures that crept silently closer, like living shadows, preparing to attack.

Moments later, the chants grew louder. "DOOMraga, DOOMraga, DOOM" echoed across the surrounding desert. But Krystallus didn't hear. He was already unconscious from strangulation.

20: CONNECTION

Bravery, I can tell you, is not the absence of fear. It is doing all you can to overcome your fear . . . as well as your fondness for life.

Smells, putrid smells. Of decay, of rancid meat, of death. The smells of the Haunted Marsh.

Krystallus opened his eyes. Yet . . . he couldn't be sure. Darkness still surrounded him, although it was a deeper, colder kind of darkness. He blinked, just to make sure his eyelids were actually open. They were—and what he saw made him wish they were not.

Shadowy forms, a shade or two darker than the thick fumes of the Marsh, floated nearby, sometimes passing directly over him. He lay in a shallow pit, a hollow filled with congealing ooze that reeked of decaying blood and bones. Sliding his body up a little higher against the boggy wall of the pit, he felt like he'd been dumped into a grave.

My own grave. He shook himself, spraying globs of muck. Watching the marsh ghouls circling, he tried to focus his eyes. But the scene kept floating back and forth, in time with the pounding ache inside his head.

He reached an unsteady hand up to his neck. The skin felt cold and clammy, as if his neck had been squeezed by frozen, deathly fingers. *The marsh ghouls*, he realized, rubbing the tender skin to bring back its warmth. *They attacked me!*

He swallowed, though it hurt. *Strangled me. Then they brought me here. Why?*

Willing his eyes to focus, he gazed at his new surroundings. Beyond the circling ghouls, he saw smoky columns of fumes and several pools of vile fluids that bubbled like boiling cauldrons. Following the rising columns, he saw the fumes widen into billowing clouds that eventually merged into a black, smoky fog so thick it blocked out the stars.

Yet somehow, there was light. Vague, pulsing, and red, like luminous blood that flowed through the swampy air.

This strange light, unlike anything he'd ever encountered, was strong enough that he could see. Or, at least, discern the shadowy layers of darkness surrounding him. Where in the Marsh did it come from? What was its source?

He tilted his head farther back, even though that angle made the pounding swell. Peering up into the gloom, he noticed an especially dark shape within the cloud, rising high above the ground. Though it was hard to be sure, the shape seemed long and cylindrical, like a gigantic worm that was standing on its base, stretching up into the sky.

Whatever it was, this shape was dark. Very dark. To the point of being a void, the utter absence of any light. Though it looked solid, it also seemed to be made of absolute emptiness.

Was it another kind of fume, thicker and darker than the

rest? He squinted, studying it closely. Suddenly he gasped, driving his fingers into the moist peat beneath him.

Alive! It's something alive! The gargantuan beast rose above him, writhing and twisting its dark body in some sort of sinister dance, an undulating column of darkness. *Great Dagda, that thing is bigger than Basilgarrad! Several times bigger. What could it be?*

As if in answer, the continuous pounding in his head started to subside—just enough that he realized that there was another pounding outside his skull. All around him, the fume-filled air was vibrating with an incessant, monotonous chant. It came from the ghouls, and also, it seemed, from the swamp itself.

"DOOMraga, DOOMraga, DOOM. DOOMraga, DOOMraga, DOOM."

The chant continued to pound, as relentless as a beating heart. Yet this couldn't have been less like a heart, with its purpose of sustaining life. No, this chant felt just the opposite, as if its purpose involved only death, destruction, and more death.

Krystallus found, in that instant, the source of the mysterious red light that permeated this part of the swamp. An eye! The beast of darkness possessed, so far up he could barely see it, a luminous red eye. Though nearly obscured by all the choking fumes, the eye shone darkly, sending a dull red glow through the fog.

Something else about the eye made Krystallus shudder. Unlike any other eye, this one pulsed to its own sinister rhythm, throbbing like an open wound. With every pulse came a wave of anger, aggression, and hatred.

All at once, he noticed an explosion of black sparks that sizzled in the air. They came from somewhere near the monster's midsection. More black sparks erupted, falling into the swamp with a chorus of hisses. Then he saw the source of the sparks.

Something is growing! Like a serpent, one made from concentrated darkness, a long black thread was emerging from the being's core. Reaching skyward, the thread surged higher and higher, groping ominously.

Krystallus watched, aghast. *What the . . . ? What is that thing?*

"DOOMraga, DOOMraga, DOOM," chanted the marsh ghouls. They tightened their circle, swooping close to the writhing beast's body. Soon they seemed to merge with its skin, shrouding the utter blackness beneath as they circled.

The monster itself continued to rock on its base, grinding its weight into the Marsh. It groaned rhythmically, in time to the ghouls' chants, all the while laboring to produce the evil thread. Meanwhile, sparks of black lightning erupted more frequently, showering the Marsh. All around Krystallus, fumes glowed with dark incandescence.

To his horror, he saw something else in the swirl of vapors near the monster's eye. Another thread! This one was reaching downward, groping like the one that had sprouted from the body of the beast. Where this second thread was coming from, Krystallus couldn't tell, but it must have been from somewhere far above, even higher than the rising fumes.

He shook his head in disbelief. His long mane, splattered with muck from the swamp, slapped against his neck. Could that new thread be stretching down from somewhere among the stars? From some source as evil as this monster of darkness?

In a flash, he understood. Whether he somehow caught an inkling of the monster's thoughts, heard another kind of language beneath its rhythmic groans, or simply guessed—he suddenly felt sure. *That new thread is coming from the Other-world. From Rhita Gawr.*

The monster released a hoarse, rasping laugh. Krystallus heard it with his ears, but also, somehow, inside his bones. Its sound, echoing through the Marsh, filled him with a heavy sense of despair. At the same time, the continuous pulse of the bloodred eye added another emotion, one he'd felt only rarely in his life. Terror.

More swirling shadows rose out of the Marsh. Whether they were ghouls or something else, Krystallus couldn't tell. But he could see them rise, like ghostly beings, toward the gap that remained between the two dark threads. Then he heard, even louder than the chants of the marsh ghouls and the groans of the monster, a sudden explosion of energy.

Black lightning blasted out of the ends of both threads. The twin currents of dark energy connected in the middle, sizzling and snapping in the swirling vapors. Tremors flowed through the surrounding fumes, while black sparks exploded everywhere. More shadows gathered, swirling around the threads like a cyclone, slowly drawing them closer.

And closer.

A huge explosion rocked the Marsh as the two dark threads connected. Vapors scattered, marsh ghouls ceased their chant, and for a brief instant the roiling fumes parted, opening to a few frail rays of starlight. Even the monster stopped writhing on its base as its hateful eye scanned the new connection.

Dark energy sizzled up and down the thread, spraying black sparks while sealing the bond. Meanwhile, the fetid fumes gathered again, deepening the darkness. But even in the gloom, one thing was certain: The two threads had joined.

"What *is* that?" Krystallus cried aloud, his caution overwhelmed by horror.

Abruptly, the pulsing red eye turned away from the dark thread—and directly toward him. For a few seconds it flashed its wrathful light upon him. Krystallus slid deeper into the shallow pit, heedless of the reeking ooze that chilled his skin and stung his nostrils.

Then, clenching his jaw, he lifted himself back up. Though he knew this monster could squash him to death in an instant, he stared back at it defiantly. He would not grovel in fear.

Doomraga's rasping laughter burst over the Marsh. It sprang from its certainty that now, at last, it had triumphed. Rhita Gawr would conquer this miserable world in the shape of a tree, just as he would conquer other worlds, as well. Now the immortal warlord was completely unstoppable! No one could possibly prevent what was about to happen—not that wretched excuse for a wizard, not that pesky green dragon, and certainly not that lowly mortal man in the pit who would soon die a most painful death.

The laughter grew louder, reverberating among the hillocks and pits of the swamp. Marsh ghouls cowered in fright, for they knew from brutal experience that when Doomraga laughed, others suffered. Creatures would soon perish. Even the ghoul who still held tight to the limp body of the hawk, that little morsel it had captured for its master's pleasure, hid itself in the darkest shadows it could find.

Doomraga ceased laughing. The towering beast's bloodshot eye swiveled, turning its gaze back to the thread. At the same time, a new sound rolled through the Marsh. Pounding and booming like a deadly drum, it began softly then steadily strengthened, swelling with every beat.

Krystallus, too, gazed at the newly connected thread. For that was the source of the drumming sound. The dark thread throbbed, bulging with some sort of terrible power that had started to flow down its length.

Abruptly, Krystallus stiffened. He knew, beyond doubt, that the power was unimaginably evil. And that it was flowing into the monster itself.

21: THE CHOICE

Doing something is usually more appealing than doing nothing. Until that something kills you.

Krystallus watched, horrified, as the dark thread throbbed. Its deep drumming, magnified by the swirling vapors, echoed across the Haunted Marsh. Just as it echoed relentlessly inside his head.

Whatever evil power flowed through that thread, pumping into the monster, spelled grave danger for Avalon. Of that Krystallus felt sure. He had no more doubt about the risk to his world than he did about his position—trapped in a shallow pit filled with rotten, reeking ooze from the swamp.

What should I do? he asked himself, digging his fingers into the bog. *No time to alert anyone powerful enough to help! Basil. Or my father, wherever he may be.*

His mud-stained brow furrowed, etching dark lines on his skin. *What,* he repeated, *should I do?* His hands closed into fists, squeezing the muck, as he realized the answer.

Whatever I can.

His eyes, as coal black as many of the shadows around him, scanned the Marsh. In the strange red glow from Doomraga's eye—now pulsing to the rhythm of the throbbing thread from the stars—he viewed the billowing fumes, the eerily bubbling pools, and the darkest shadows that were, he knew, marsh ghouls.

He frowned, thinking what an utter fool he'd been to imagine that those wicked creatures might still have a shred of goodness left inside them. Sure, they had actually helped his father once, in the quest for the magical Mirror. But that was centuries ago, and even more centuries after their terrible sacrifice to keep their precious lands away from Rhita Gawr—still mortal in those days, but every bit the brutal warlord he remained now.

What a bitter irony that those very creatures had ended up serving Rhita Gawr! How far they had fallen from the proud and powerful enchantresses they once were, who took commands from no one but themselves. *No*, thought Krystallus, *I won't get any help from them.*

His jaw tightened with resolve. *But I might be able to evade them.* Right now, while the ghouls were still hiding, trying to avoid any attention from the monster, he had an opportunity to do something bold. Something that no sane person would even consider.

I'm going to attack this beast. While there's still time.

He felt, hidden under his mud-crusted tunic, the dagger in the sheath attached to his belt. It wouldn't be much use against a monster as enormous as this one. But it was, at least, as sharp as any blade in Avalon, having been wrought by the elven swordsmiths of Ultan Fairlyn at the height of their skills.

In fact, he now recalled, the master swordsmith had told him that this dagger could pierce "even a hide hardened by magic"—even though it would be wielded by a man with no magic of his own.

Well, now, he thought as he patted the blade, *this will be your chance.*

He peered up at the gargantuan figure towering over him. Like a column of solid darkness, the monster rose into the swirling vapors, its red eye flashing high above the swamp. The dark thread continued to throb, pushing some horrendous substance into the monster's body. What could that substance be? What evil power would it give to this beast? And how much time remained before the monster would become so powerful that nothing could possibly stop it?

I'd rather not find out. He grimaced, wiping a chunk of mud off his chin. *Which is why,* he told himself with determination, *I'm going to try to cut that thread.*

Slowly and silently, he lifted himself out of the pit, careful not to alert the cowering ghouls. Rancid liquid, unnaturally cold and full of decaying scraps of flesh and bone, sloshed against his tunic and leggings; thick muck sucked on his boots, nearly tugging them loose as he moved. But he barely noticed. All his attention was concentrated on the huge monster he hoped to climb, much as he'd climbed the misty cliffs of Eagles' Canyon.

Except this time, the cliff would be alive. And brimming with vengeance and wrath.

Krystallus started to crawl over to the monster's base. Moving as stealthily as a ghoul himself, he made every effort to blend with the surrounding shadows. All it would take, he knew, was a single mistake and a hoard of marsh ghouls— or worse—would descend on him. Then he would never succeed in his goal to disrupt the flow of evil into the dark beast. Never do his part to save Avalon. And never see Serella again.

That last goal, the most personal, made him swallow. Worse than the bitter taste of the Marsh in his mouth was the terrible prospect of losing everything he shared with Serella. But he knew that, unless he succeeded in this wild attempt, Avalon would soon be doomed. So he would lose it all in any case. Besides, Serella would completely understand his purpose in trying . . . just as she would commend his spirit of adventure. After all, wasn't she even now planning to return to Shadowroot? She had ignored all his pleas to stay away from that realm, hoping to solve the mystery of the plague her people called *darkdeath*.

As Krystallus crept closer, the terrible thread continued to throb—drumming, drumming, drumming. The Marsh itself vibrated with every beat of the deadly drum. The oozing muck shook under his open hands, sliding through his fingers. Vile pools shuddered to the rhythm of the pounding.

He changed course, slipping behind some twisted stalks of swamp grass. Right in front of him, only partly visible in the dim red light, crouched a marsh ghoul. Though it lay in a low trench, cowering from its master, he'd seen it stir suspiciously as he approached. He waited, heart slamming against his ribs, watching the ghoul. After a tense moment, it seemed to forget about him, lowering itself deeper into the trench.

Cautiously, he started to crawl again, keeping as far away as possible from that ghoul while staying alert for others. Like a shifting piece of night, he slid across the surface of the swamp. Bit by bit, he drew nearer to his goal, ever aware that time was dwindling.

The monster, meanwhile, continued to writhe on its base, swaying with the incessant pumping. Black lightning exploded along the length of the thread, crackling and sizzling with dark energy. All the while, the drumbeat pounded, making the entire swamp shiver.

Krystallus paused, only a short distance away. He could see the monster's base, a wrinkled mass of darkness, as it rocked within a pit that sloshed with some sort of fluid. Taking a sniff, he scowled. *That pit reeks of decomposing corpses. Where did they come from?*

Pushing that thought aside, his mind turned to more pressing questions. What would it feel like to touch the monster's horrid skin? Could he grip it securely enough to climb, despite the constant swaying? Would the monster feel him, or be so preoccupied with the pumping that it might not notice?

He drew an uncertain breath. *Time to find out.*

As silent as a shadow, he slid into the monster's pit. The wretched fluid tugged at his leggings and assaulted his sense of smell. Yet he stayed focused. For several seconds, he watched the monster's base sloshing back and forth in the fluid, trying to gauge its motion. At last, choosing the instant, he lunged—

Onto the base! The skin felt cold but flexible and easy to

grasp. Finding plenty of climbing holds in the saggy skin, he began to work his way higher. Moving steadily but stealthily, he quickly rose above the worst stench. Pausing for a glance at what lay above, he saw the beast swaying against the fumes, its immense body rising impossibly high. Far overhead, he gazed at the dark thread, lit by ominous sparks.

I must get up there. Before it's too late.

For an instant, the swaying vista made him feel dizzy. He looked away, concentrating on his hands, tinted red by the monster's glowing eye, and on the utterly lightless skin beneath. That skin felt increasingly cold, but not in the usual sense. For it arose not from a chilly temperature, but from the absence of any temperature at all. This cold came from sheer negativity.

He reached for a new handhold and continued to ascend. Quivers ran down the monster's body with each throbbing pulse of the thread. Yet despite those tremors and the beast's constant swaying, Krystallus made progress. Carefully choosing his holds to avoid any sudden slips that might alert the monster of his presence, he rose higher.

And higher.

And still higher.

Breathing heavily, he stopped to assess his progress. He glanced up at the place where the dark thread connected. Very close! He would reach that junction in just a few moments—a good thing, since his fingers felt strangely numb.

He removed a hand from the monster's skin, working his fingers. The numbness persisted. Grimly, he reached into his tunic to touch his sketchbook. Its familiar leathery texture, together with its comparative warmth, brought back a hint of feeling. But he knew that his own skin couldn't tolerate much more contact with the monster. Or else he wouldn't be able to hold his dagger when the time came.

Soon, he told himself. *I'll be there soon.*

Again he turned his gaze upward, preparing to climb. Suddenly he noticed something strange. Terribly strange. Squinting to make sure he was really seeing such a thing, he peered closely.

Krystallus gasped. For he was, indeed, seeing correctly.

The monster's body had started to change.

22: CYCLOPS

People reveal a lot about themselves by how they enter a place.
And even more by how they leave.

Transfixed, Krystallus stared up at this strange new sight. Where the throbbing thread joined the monster's body, the skin had started to bubble, ripple, and bulge.

This beast is transforming! Anxiously, he chewed his lip. *Into . . . what?*

Thoughts of other matters—his numb fingers, the monster's constant swaying, even the need to hurry—vanished. All he could do was stare, gaping, at the bubbling expansion of skin. The beast's entire midsection was now swelling steadily.

Black lightning crackled all along the thread, which continued its relentless pulse, pounding in time to the flashing eye. Whatever that thread was pumping into the monster's body was rapidly filling it. And changing it.

Faster than Krystallus would have thought possible, the monster's whole upper half was expanding into an immense, powerful chest. Near the top, two stubs appeared from swiftly developing shoulders. Quickly, the stubs stretched outward, fast becoming muscular arms. At the very top, a gargantuan head was forming—a head with a single, pulsing red eye.

No longer shaped like a massive leech, whose wormlike body bore no appendages, the monster was rapidly transforming into something more dangerous. More mobile. And, Krystallus felt certain, more powerful.

It looks like . . . a troll! A huge, one-eyed troll. Unbidden, an image popped into his mind—a creature from one of the myths he'd heard as a child, a story from that place called Greece on Earth. He searched his mind for the creature's name.

Cyclops—that was it.

Suddenly, the monster's skin beneath him started to crease, then pull apart, dividing down the middle. Into legs!

Just as the skin separated with a terrible tearing sound, Krystallus leaped to one side. Groping with fingers now thoroughly numb from the cold, he tried to latch on to a massive, newly forming thigh. Desperately, he clawed at the skin, as dark as the void, hoping to catch some sort of hold that could bear his weight.

Nothing! He started to slip, sliding downward with increasing speed. High as he was above the Marsh, he knew that if he fell, he would surely die—either from the impact or from the wrathful marsh ghouls. And he would never have another chance to help Avalon.

Just before he lost all control and toppled over backward, his feet struck a ledge. He slammed down in a heap. Picking himself up, even as the ledge expanded beneath him, he realized what it was.

The troll's kneecap. Staring up at the muscular thigh above him, and the throbbing thread that now entered the beast's belly, he could see that precious little time remained. If he was still going to cut that thread—in the hope that it might reduce the troll's power, or at least keep the troll from becoming invulnerable—he needed to do it immediately.

He started to climb again, faster than ever. Despite his numb hands and the swelling body beneath him, he ascended rapidly. Like a tiny spider crawling up a vast, undulating wall, he drew nearer to his goal.

Sparks of negative energy fell around him, hissing as they passed through the vapors that rose from the swamp. One spark landed on his shoulder, burning coldly as it opened a hole in the cloth. He flicked it off with a numb hand, then kept climbing.

The troll, meanwhile, grew more defined. From the ends of the great arms grew strong, three-fingered hands. The shoulders swelled mightily, merging into a thick, sturdy neck. Below the lone eye appeared an immense mouth filled with jagged teeth. Then the mouth opened and released a loud roar that crashed through the Marsh, reminding all the ghouls just who they served.

The force of that roar almost knocked Krystallus off his perch. He reeled, barely holding on to a rippling muscle near the top of the thigh. Jamming his feet into a crease, he regained his balance.

Yet he felt no relief. For something in the troll's outburst had spawned a new thought, one that conveyed the full extent of Avalon's peril. It was only a guess. But the guess was so terrifying he fervently hoped it wasn't true.

This troll wasn't merely being fueled by the magic of Rhita Gawr. Much worse—this troll *was* Rhita Gawr. The physical embodiment of the spirit warlord. He was coming to Avalon! He was using that dark thread to flow down into the monster, using its body as his own.

Instantly, Krystallus started climbing again. Now every fraction of a second mattered more than ever. *I must cut that cord!*

The troll roared again. Stretching his huge arms skyward, the towering warrior squeezed his fists and bellowed with both triumph and revenge. For he could feel his power steadily growing, already overwhelming that leechlike minion who had served him so well—and who, now that the crucial tasks had been completed, no longer needed to exist.

Rhita Gawr's face turned up to the stars, toward the deep well of darkness where his journey had begun. He had waited many long years to return, in mortal form, to this world between worlds. Avalon—how he'd longed for it, lusted for it! He would soon turn its abundant magic to achieving his ultimate goal: conquering all the worlds.

He stamped one of his enormous, newly grown feet in the Marsh. Muck, decaying flesh, and rotten fluid sprayed every-where. All that, along with sparks of black lightning, rained down on the backs of the cowering ghouls.

Rhita Gawr's wide mouth slavered, sending a river of drool down his chin. He could almost taste, at last, the fruits of his labors—fruits so precious that the mere possibility of gaining them had sustained him through centuries of warfare, hardship, and humiliation. Victory. Conquest. Destruction of all his enemies, in this world and others.

His monstrous eye flashed, tinting the noxious fumes blood red. Nothing, he knew, could stop him now. The dark thread continued to fill him with power—immortal power. In just a few more minutes, he would be absolutely invincible—strong enough to bring his rule to Avalon, and brutal enough to vanquish anyone foolish enough to try to oppose him.

He opened his mouth to roar triumphantly again. But just as he started, the noise died in his throat. He then bellowed, not in triumph but in rage, shaking the entire swamp with the force of his wrath.

His enemy! He sensed the nearness of his foe, eager to attack. His eye, blazing with fury, roved all around. Wherever that enemy was right now, painful death would follow.

Krystallus, clinging to the troll's body, felt the red glare of the eye fall upon him. Uncontrollably, he shuddered. Had he been discovered? So close to his goal?

The eye, however, moved past him. It turned, burning with hatred, toward the far side of the Marsh where clouds of fumes rose skyward. Krystallus, too, looked in that direction, following the troll's gaze.

Basilgarrad! Wings spread wide, carrying Merlin himself, the great green dragon burst through the clouds. He flew straight at the monstrous troll—and into battle.

23: ATTACKS

A dragon's scales may be thick, but they can't stop the arrows of grief.

Basilgarrad tore through the thick, billowing fumes that shrouded the Marsh. He could feel Merlin, who rode atop his enormous head, shifting in anticipation. Simultaneously, he felt his own body tense, from his powerful jaws down to the knob of his tail. For he, like the wizard, knew that they soared into battle—the ultimate battle for Avalon.

Shredding the dark vapors, the dragon noticed a pulsing red glow that permeated the fumes ahead. He knew, even without seeing the source of the glow, exactly where it came from. *That's the monster's eye, I'm certain.*

Merlin nodded, having heard his companion's thoughts. His beard, blown back by the wind, flapped against Basilgarrad's ear—hard enough that the owl Euclid screeched and leaped from the beard into the pocket of the wizard's robe.

"Basil, old chap . . . ," Merlin began. Although he spoke directly into the dragon's ear, he needed to raise his voice to be heard above the whistling wind. "Somehow I don't think our worst problem is the monster of the Marsh."

"What?" demanded the dragon, scrunching his snout in surprise as he flew. "He's the agent of Rhita Gawr. What could possibly be worse?"

"Rhita Gawr himself!" the wizard shouted. "I have a terrible feeling in my gut." The wind tore at his words. "A feeling I've had only a few times in my life, when I've faced that tyrant in person."

Basilgarrad, beating his wide wings, growled deep in his throat. "I've learned to trust those feelings. But how could Rhita Gawr himself have come here from the spirit realm?"

"Unlike Dagda, he has no qualms about trying. And something tells me he's found a way."

The dragon's mighty wings slapped at the foul-smelling fumes. Abruptly, his ears tilted forward, almost dislodging the wizard. But Basilgarrad didn't notice Merlin's cry of surprise, for he'd focused all his attention on the relentless drumming sound that came from somewhere ahead.

"There!" he cried as they burst through a curtain of clouds.

Straight ahead loomed a towering warrior in the shape of a troll, his torso connected to a cord that reached skyward. The troll's entire body seemed to be made of concentrated darkness. At the instant they ripped through the clouds, he trained his lone eye on them, flooding them with its wrathful red glow.

"That cord," rumbled Basilgarrad. "It's throbbing with some sort of magic."

"Right!" answered Merlin, lifting his head to follow the

dark thread's route up to the stars. "The magic of Rhita Gawr."

"Well, then," the dragon replied with a flare of his nostrils, "I can tell you this: Rhita Gawr smells worse than horrible! He reeks of troll armpits, swamp rot, and more."

The wizard scowled. "This is no time for you to show off your useless sense of smell. Concentrate on your attack plan!"

"I am, don't worry." Basilgarrad added, under his breath, "But that drooling bully really needs a bath."

Accelerating his speed, the dragon allowed himself one brief glance behind, catching a glimpse of the smaller, luminous blue dragon who followed him. *Stay clear, Marnya*, he thought, fervently hoping she would value her safety as much as he did. Seeing the tiny young dragon who flapped madly to keep up with her, he added, *And you, too, Ganta.*

"YOU DARE TO ATTACK ME!" roared the troll. The force of his voice shredded clouds and rocked the swamp.

"We do!" boomed Basilgarrad, his roar almost as loud. "For you attack Avalon!"

Krystallus, having climbed up to the troll's waist, sucked in his breath. *They're here! Basil—and also my father! But they'll need some help.*

He continued to climb. Only a small distance remained before he would reach the base of the thread. Heedless of the black sparks that rained down on his back, he kept moving higher, closer to the cord. He didn't know whether his dagger could pierce it, only that he must try.

The troll pivoted on his massive legs, turning to face the approaching dragon. But as he turned, the cord tugged forcefully against him. Suddenly realizing that the throbbing thread restricted his own mobility—and, as long as he remained attached to it, increased his vulnerability—the warrior scowled.

He needed just a few more minutes . . . and his power would be complete, his triumph guaranteed. In that glorious instant, the cord would dissolve. And his reign of conquest would begin.

He stamped one of his enormous feet in the Marsh. Reeking fluid and muck sprayed high into the air, while tremors coursed through the swamp. "Arise, my ghouls!" he commanded. "Stop these intruders!"

Like a flock of menacing shadows, the marsh ghouls immediately rose up from the swamp. They glided through the billowing fumes, tightening their formation. Then, as if they were a single blot of darkness, they flew straight into the path of the oncoming dragon.

Wild shrieks erupted from the charging ghouls. Basilgarrad roared angrily, with such force that some of them veered aside. But most of them attacked ferociously, hurling themselves at his wings, chest, and head. Although his élano-hardened scales easily repelled their blows, the ghouls swarmed so thickly around his face that he couldn't see anything but swirling shadows.

"Out of my way!" he bellowed.

But the marsh ghouls only intensified their swarm.

Roaring with frustration, Basilgarrad did what he least wanted to do—slow down. Otherwise he risked flying right into the troll's massive fists, or even that drooling mouth. He tilted his wings backward, slowing his charge, then swooped lower to try to shake free of the ghouls. Although he flew low enough to scrape the swamp's brittle grass with his claws, the shadowy beasts continued to crowd around his head.

The dragon veered sharply sideways, trying to fly with only brief glimpses through the mass of ghouls. *Can't you do something?* he called telepathically to Merlin. *I can't shake these pests. And that gives Rhita Gawr more time!*

But the wizard was too busy to answer. He swung his staff wildly, trying to swat marsh ghouls out of the sky. Though they usually evaded his blows, every so often he connected. A volley of sparks exploded from the staff, tearing the ghoul to shreds of black vapor. Yet only an instant later, the ghoul reformed, unifying the shreds, and attacked again.

I'm doing my best, answered Merlin at last. His swinging staff whooshed through the air by Basilgarrad's ear. *My very best.*

That's not good enough! the dragon replied, veering blindly from one side to the other.

Truth is . . . , began Merlin before he paused to take several swings in rapid succession, *nothing I'm doing works. These ghouls are not very smart—but they are indestructible. There's no way to defeat them!*

"Find a way!" roared the dragon. "We're losing precious time."

Indeed, at that moment, Rhita Gawr burst into vengeful laughter that boomed across the Marsh. "You cannot even find me, dragon," he taunted. "How did you ever hope to fight me?"

He watched the swerving flight of his foe who couldn't break free of the ghouls, then laughed again. "When we do fight," he declared with a glance upward at the throbbing thread's source, "you will regret this delay. And your folly to think you could ever defeat me."

While all this was happening, Marnya and Ganta flew nearer, slicing through the curtains of noxious fumes. Instantly, they saw Basilgarrad's peril. Through the swirling vapors above the swamp, the two smaller dragons eyed each other.

"Go help Basil," Marnya commanded. "Do anything you can to distract those ghouls."

"I will," the young dragon piped valiantly. He hovered, flapping his thin wings.

Her azure eyes turned to the troll, who was watching Basilgarrad so intently that he hadn't yet noticed her amidst the fumes. She glared at him icily. "That beast looks entirely too pleased with himself."

Ganta's face creased in a grin. "Go unplease him, mistress Marnya."

She nodded. "I will. Now remember," she said with a cautionary wave of her flipper, "those ghouls are deadly."

"Not to me," he retorted. With a spiraling turn, he spun around and zipped toward the enemy.

Marnya, for her part, banked a wide turn through the billowing gases, coming around behind the troll. To give herself maximum control, she spread her flippers to their widest. Hoping to catch her foe off guard, she dived straight at his back.

Just before she reached his hulking body, she veered upward, skimming past the back of his hairless head. Marnya raised her tail—not nearly as hefty as Basilgarrad's, but still a potent weapon. Then, with all the strength she'd gained from a lifetime of propelling herself through the ocean by whipping her tail, she slammed it down on the troll's skull.

Splat! The sharp blow echoed across the Marsh. Instantly, thick black fluid—so dark it seemed like liquid night—oozed from the gash on the troll's skin.

Marnya nodded with satisfaction. *Basil,* she thought, *would be pleased.* She glanced anxiously at the heavy fumes that nearly hid him from view. *I just wish he'd hurry and get over here. Until then—.*

Her thought ended with Rhita Gawr's deafening roar.

24: A WORLD WE CHERISHED

*Many times in my long life, I wished I could know the future.
Then came that particular time, when I couldn't bear to think
about the future at all.*

AAAAARRRGGHH!" bellowed Rhita Gawr. His cry
blew through the Marsh like a forceful gale, scattering
fumes and emptying pools.

Seething with anger, the troll whirled around, fast enough
that he nearly tangled his brawny arms in the cord attached
to his belly. His rage was so intense that he didn't even notice
the small figure of Krystallus, barely hanging on at the base
of the cord. No, Rhita Gawr's mind was fixed on one goal—
finding the creature who had dared to attack him by slashing
the back of his head. His malevolent eye searched the sky,
blazing angrily.

Thrown out of his climbing holds when the troll had
turned so violently, Krystallus had lunged for the only thing
he could reach—the cord itself. Somehow wrapping his arms
around the dark thread, he managed to hoist himself up onto
it. Straddling the cord with his legs, he felt it continue to
throb beneath him, pumping immortal strength into the troll.

Krystallus steadied himself, drew a deep breath, and then reached for his dagger.

Only a few seconds earlier, Merlin had remembered something crucial. Suddenly hitting on a new strategy to disperse the marsh ghouls, he ceased swinging his staff and drew it to his side. Leaning his back against Basilgarrad's upright ear, he raised his face to the swarming ghouls.

"Hear me," he cried. "It is I, Merlin, who speaks to you. Do you not remember our first meeting, back in the days of Fincayra's magical Mirror? We are friends, not enemies! You saved my life, and I won your freedom. Let us be allies once more—in this new world of Avalon."

Several of the ghouls stopped shrieking and shook themselves, as if awakening from a long and terrible dream. They hovered above Merlin, not attacking—but also not withdrawing. Basilgarrad, meanwhile, flew in wide circles above the swamp. Still unable to see more than a shred of his surroundings, he roared with utter frustration.

Merlin, though, kept speaking in a calm, measured tone to the ghouls. "We shared a world, you and I. A world we prized—even more, a world we cherished! Help me again, my friends. Rise up to your better, wiser, truer selves. The selves I once knew. Join me once more, this time to save Avalon!"

The hovering ghouls started to pull away. Several of them drew back far enough that, for the first time since their swarm had descended, Basilgarrad had a clear view of the swamp. He'd flown some distance away from Rhita Gawr, so that the troll's huge body was only barely visible through the swirling fumes. But that fact did not diminish his joy at being able to see again. And mount an attack, at last.

Not bad, he told Merlin telepathically.

Well, I just—began the wizard. But his thought ended abruptly when the troll bellowed in rage at Marnya's unexpected blow. The troll's outburst sent tremors through the Marsh.

All at once, the retreating ghouls halted and shrieked with fright. Believing that their all-powerful master had bellowed at them for pulling away, they instantly dived again at Basilgarrad and Merlin. They swarmed more intensely than ever, hurling themselves at the dragon's eyes to obstruct his vision.

"No!" shouted Basilgarrad, forced again to spin in aimless circles over the Marsh.

"Curses!" yelled Merlin. He swatted a pair of attacking ghouls with his staff. "I'm sorry, Basil. These wretched creatures are most driven by their fear of Rhita Gawr."

The dragon gasped. A new idea flashed across his mind, bright as a bolt of lightning. *What if . . .*

At that same instant, young Ganta flew up to the mass of marsh ghouls that was shrouding his uncle's vision. Anger coursed through his veins. He must do something! Immediately! But what?

His eyes reddened with rage. These ghouls needed to vanish. To stop interfering with the battle. All of Avalon was at stake! Just then, he felt a new rumbling down inside his chest.

His breath grew hot, his throat tightened—and Ganta did something he'd never done before.

He breathed fire! Though it was only a tiny spurt of flame, so small that it wasn't even noticed by the marsh ghouls, to Ganta it seemed like a gigantic conflagration, big enough to burn a whole realm.

Meanwhile, Basilgarrad put his new idea to work. Using his power to conjure smells, he created a terribly potent one. Part rancid armpit, part pungent swamp, and part unwashed troll—the smell reeked powerfully. And greatly resembled Rhita Gawr's mortal form.

The marsh ghouls suddenly squealed in terror, thinking they had accidentally attacked their master. Instantly, they scattered to all ends of the swamp. Burrowing themselves into pits and plunging into pools, they cowered in fear of Rhita Gawr's unending wrath.

Merlin, wide-eyed, nodded in approval. *Now, Basil, it's my turn to be impressed.*

The dragon snorted. *Just don't call my skill with smells "useless."*

Never again, old chap.

Basilgarrad spun around, working his mighty wings. To his surprise, Ganta was flying nearby. He gave his small but feisty nephew a wink.

"I did it, master Basil!" piped the young dragon. He flapped his wings enthusiastically and bobbed his little head. "I scared off the ghouls. With my breath of fire!"

Only half hearing, Basilgarrad nodded. "I'm sure you

did." Then he beat his wings, charging straight at the enemy he was longing to fight—and soon, to defeat.

His enormous body tore through the fumes. Shredded vapors trailed from his jagged wing tips, his deadly claws, and his massive tail. Merlin, ready for action, crouched atop the dragon's head. Both of them knew that now, at last, they would face Rhita Gawr. And that their battle would determine the fate of Avalon.

As they burst through the last curtain of clouds, the troll stood in clear view. But Rhita Gawr's attention was not turned toward them. Rather, his entire wrath was directed at another foe, a more slender dragon whose luminous blue scales gleamed even in the darkness of the swamp.

Marnya! Seeing her made Basilgarrad's heart leap—not with joy, but with dread. For she was flying perilously close to the troll, barely dodging the savage swipes of his hands.

"Be careful!" shouted Basilgarrad. He pumped his wings, accelerating to his greatest speed.

The flying water dragon didn't hear the warning. She continued to spin around the troll's head, nearly grazing one of his ears. As she swooped past, she flicked her tail, slicing the troll's earlobe.

Rhita Gawr roared in uncontrollable rage while black fluid oozed from his wound. Clearly pleased with her success, Marnya slowed down just enough to take a brief glance at what she'd done. At the same time, her foe's red eye flashed vengefully—and marked her trajectory. Before she could speed up again, the troll swung his huge fist.

"No!" cried Basilgarrad.

"Look out!" shouted Merlin.

Their cries combined with Marnya's scream and the sound of crushing bones as Rhita Gawr's fist slammed into her body. She tumbled from the sky, spiraling down into the swamp.

25: MERLIN'S DILEMMA

Of all the things I've wished for, two stand above the rest: a clearer understanding of the choices I was making . . . and a little more time to make them.

Marnya!" shouted Basilgarrad. His voice echoed around the Marsh in a broken, distorted refrain.

He tilted his wings and started to veer down to the spot where she had fallen, a bubbling pool shrouded by sheets of dark vapors. At that instant, Merlin tugged on the edge of his ear. "Not now, Basil!"

"I must go to her," the dragon moaned.

"Later," pleaded the wizard. "Listen, I know how you feel. Believe me, I do! But we have only seconds left to stop that troll. Before it gains all the power coming down that cord—all the power of Rhita Gawr!"

Basilgarrad hesitated, but continued to swoop downward. His eyes, usually glowing so bright, seemed as shadowed as the surrounding swamp. "Can't . . . leave her. Can't . . . lose her."

Though Merlin's eyes grew misty from his friend's plight, he pounded his staff on the dragon's head. "Basil, this is our last chance! We must fight!"

The great dragon ground his many rows of teeth. "No," he declared. "*You* must fight. I will go . . . to her."

"All right," agreed Merlin grudgingly. "But first get me to the cord. As fast as you can!"

Basilgarrad swooped upward again. Beating his powerful wings, he growled, "Get ready."

"Ready?" asked the wizard. "For what?"

"For your chance to fly on your own."

"My *what*?"

Basilgarrad nodded as his wings pumped. "This way, you might get to the cord without being seen." He tore through the fumes, steadily gaining speed. "And without drawing me into the fight."

"But, Basil—"

Abruptly, the dragon slammed both his wings backward, halting his flight in midair. At the same time, he whipped his neck forward, hurling Merlin into the vapors. The wizard suddenly flew—his arms flailing, his robe flapping, and his beard blown backward by the wind. He sailed straight at the dark thread that connected the troll to the sky above—and at the troll himself. Fortunately, Rhita Gawr's lone eye was turned elsewhere, at the spot where Marnya had fallen.

Merlin shot toward the cord. As the wind whistled past, he judged his altitude to be about halfway between the troll's belly and the pulsing eye. *If I can just grab that cord,* he thought, *I'll be near enough to inflict some damage.*

Euclid, who had been hiding in a deep pocket, poked out his head. Seeing that the wizard was flying through the air, he shrieked in horror. Then, seeing their destination, he shrieked again. Furiously working his little wings, he wriggled out of the pocket and into the air where he could control his own flight.

An instant later, Merlin struck the cord. Like a windblown moth landing on a branch, he hit hard and clung tight, even though his momentum nearly threw him past. Wrapping his arms and legs around the thread, he hung on, trying to keep himself from falling. Though he slid some ways down the length, he finally steadied himself. Breathlessly, he leaned his forehead against the cord.

I feel it pumping! He knew that every throb made his enemy stronger. In a matter of seconds, Rhita Gawr would be unstoppable.

He lifted his head, knowing what he must do. Peering up at the thick vapors that obscured the stars, he could see the outlines of the troll's muscular shoulders and angular jaw. Both were lit by the ominous glow of the bloodred eye, which continued to flash in time to the pulsing thread.

That eye, thought Merlin grimly, *is his weakest point. And my only hope.*

Taking one hand off the cord, he pulled his staff from his belt. Firmly, he grasped the staff, just below its twisted, knotted top. His voice a bare whisper, he spoke to it as he would have spoken to an old friend.

"I need you now, Ohnyalei, more than ever before. I need you to gather all the power you have. Every last spark, whatever you can muster. For even that," he added with a glance at the glowing eye far above, "might not be enough."

The staff quivered, trembling in his hand. Then, like a subtle dawn, its top began to glow ever so slightly. Soon a faint, silvery aura surrounded it.

Merlin watched it closely, between anxious glances skyward. He never noticed, far below by the troll's waist, the other person who also clung to the throbbing cord.

Krystallus, for his part, never looked up—and certainly never realized that, if he had, he would have seen his father, preparing to strike a blow with the staff. Indeed, Krystallus was busy striking blows of his own, working feverishly to pierce the dark thread with his dagger. Sweat dripped from his face and hands, while his arm muscles ached from the strain. Yet so far he had just barely scraped the thread's tough surface.

Where is Basil? And my father? he wondered, wiping his sweaty brow with the sleeve of his tunic. *And what happened to that other dragon who was doing so well at harassing this monster?*

At that very moment, Basilgarrad was dragging Marnya's limp body out of the reeking pool where she had fallen. Gently clasping her fin between his teeth, he tugged to free her from the pool. Although the ooze sucked at her body, his great strength prevailed. He dragged her onto soggy but more solid ground, then somberly gazed at her.

Clumps of peat and decaying flesh covered her face; black muck streaked her once-radiant scales. Her azure eyes lay hidden behind closed lids. Far worse, though, was her utter stillness—the stillness of death. She did not breathe, or blink, or moan.

Basilgarrad lifted his massive head to the sky, stretching his neck upward, and bellowed in pain. It was an anguished sound, terrible to hear for all its pain. For no sound ever heard in Avalon carried more suffering than the sobs of a dragon.

Nearby, in the shadows, sat Ganta, his little wings folded against his back. All the joy of breathing fire had vanished. Instead, he wondered how the fire of life, especially in someone so fully alive, could end so quickly.

Several tears, as dark as the billowing fumes of the swamp, fell from Basilgarrad's eyes. Down his face they rolled, sliding over his scales, then down his long neck all the way to his shoulders. There, catching sparks of green light from his eyes, they dropped. Still glinting, they landed on Marnya's lifeless throat.

"Marvelous!" boomed the troll, his voice rising in raucous laughter. "I would kill that insect again, if I could. Just to see you suffer."

Basilgarrad, consumed with sorrow, didn't respond, or even look up. He merely stroked the contours of Marnya's face with his wing tip.

"Did you not hear me?" thundered Rhita Gawr. "Are you deaf, or just cowardly?"

When Basilgarrad still did not reply, the troll glared at him. Enraged, he stepped toward the mourning dragon. But the cord held him back, preventing him from taking more than a single stride. With a roar of frustration, he stamped his huge feet in the swamp, splattering mud and fluids. Because he continued to fix his pulsing eye on Basilgarrad, he didn't notice the two much smaller figures hanging from the cord itself.

Merlin, hoping his staff was finally ready, gazed into its silvery glow. "Is that everything you have?" he whispered. "We will need it all."

He watched as the staff's top glowed a bit brighter, crackling with energy. "All right, then." He raised the staff and started to point it at the troll's evil eye. "Send your mightiest blast to—"

Rhita Gawr suddenly bellowed in surprise, stopping the wizard from finishing his command. In that instant, Merlin turned and saw exactly what his foe had seen. Krystallus! Down at the junction of the cord and the troll's belly, Krystallus sat holding a dagger, trying to sever the connection.

By the breath of Dagda, that brave lad! thought Merlin, just as surprised as the troll.

His roar of surprise quickly turning to fury, Rhita Gawr reached down with a massive hand and plucked up Krystallus. He pinched the struggling man's chest between his thumb and forefinger, so hard that Krystallus gasped for breath and dropped his dagger. The blade plunged downward, bounced off the troll's knee, then fell into the bog below.

As Rhita Gawr lifted him higher, toward a drooling mouth filled with jagged teeth, Krystallus passed very close to Merlin. Seeing his father suspended from the cord, Krystallus opened his eyes wide with astonishment. For a brief moment, their gazes met—two pairs of coal-black eyes that had not looked at each other for years. In that moment, both father and son saw more than they had believed possible.

Merlin, still holding his staff above his head, hesitated. His tufted eyebrows lifted to their highest. *Should I blast the troll's eye or help Krystallus? Try to save Avalon—or my son?*

Seeing the consternation on his father's face, Krystallus immediately guessed the wizard's thoughts—and dilemma. "No, Father!" he croaked, barely able to breathe. "Forget about me. Kill this beast!"

Rhita Gawr's immense mouth slavered as he carried his victim higher. "I will eat you, worm. Devour you!"

Still Merlin hesitated, as if he'd been frozen in time. He knew what he should do. Avalon needed him to seize this moment, this final chance, to save it from Rhita Gawr's domination. The staff he held right now was not just a weapon, but the last hope for their world.

Besides, Krystallus was not really someone deserving special treatment. He was, in fact, someone whose words had cut deeper than any sword. Who had done everything possible to distance himself. Who had, more than anyone else, hurt the wizard's heart.

Who is, Merlin told himself, *my son.* He bit his lip. *And he is right! He knows that he must die—so that Avalon might live.*

In a trembling voice, he said quietly, "I'm sorry, Krystallus. Very sorry."

He grimaced, watching for another instant as his son approached the troll's drooling mouth. Then, his decision made, he aimed his glowing staff and spoke the command:

"Save him. Save my son!"

A fiery bolt of lightning shot from the top of the staff, sizzling on its arc through the air. It struck the troll's hand, just below the knuckles—not hard enough to destroy the monster's flesh, but to singe it. Rhita Gawr roared in sudden pain, opened his burned hand, and dropped Krystallus.

So bright was the dazzling flash, it illuminated the whole marsh and, for a brief instant, dispersed the many layers of shadows. Even as Rhita Gawr roared from the burn, he was forced to shut his eye as he reeled from the brilliant flash— which prevented him from seeing what happened next.

Merlin leaped off the throbbing cord. Carried aloft by his still-glowing staff, he flew up to catch Krystallus. There! The wizard wrapped one arm around his son's waist, holding him tight, as the hairs of his unruly beard mingled with those of the younger man's flowing mane.

In a last burst of power, the darkening staff carried them both downward. Just as they landed in a boggy pool some distance away from the troll, the staff sputtered, sparkled one more time, then finally extinguished. Darkness once again filled the Marsh, lit only by the pulsing red glow of Rhita Gawr's reopened eye far above their heads.

Merlin used the staff to steady himself as he stood in the muck of the pool. He slid his fingers along the staff, now as dark as the fumes rising around them, fully aware that its power was spent. It would take, he knew, quite some time for its magic to restore itself. Just as he knew that he no longer could do anything to stop Rhita Gawr. Yet he still, somehow, felt sure he'd made the right choice.

Peering at the staff, whose edges dimly gleamed with the red glow, he whispered, "Thanks, my friend."

Krystallus, who was standing in a deeper part of the pool, stepped toward his father. His boots squelched in the mud as he approached, his face entirely a scowl. "You shouldn't have done that."

Merlin nodded. "I know."

"That was stupid." Krystallus brushed a clump of peat off his nose. "Really stupid."

"Yes, I know." The wizard ran a hand through his mud-stained beard. He paused, as Euclid's feathery form dived out of the sky and back into the nest. Then, gazing at his son, Merlin added, "But as you know well . . . it wasn't the first time I've done something stupid."

Krystallus gazed back. His scowl started to melt away, for he'd clearly heard the note of apology. "I guess," he replied, "that runs in our family."

Far above them, Rhita Gawr roared angrily. "Where are you, worm? When I find you, I will crush you, maim you, skin you, and devour you!"

His bloodred eye, seething with rage, searched around the swamp. But the two small humans down in the murky pool, shrouded as they were by dark fumes, eluded him. Bellowing with wrath, the troll tugged at the cord that kept him from moving—and from completing his long-awaited conquest of Avalon.

The dark thread pulsed once more, pumping the final drops of power into his body. Then, all at once, the cord started to dissolve. Black sparks exploded all along its length, hissing and crackling in the vapors. The whole thread, stretching all the way up to the empty place between the stars, disintegrated. Only one trace of it remained: a thin trail of black sparks that hung in the air, crackling ominously.

Rhita Gawr roared in triumph. He was, at last, completely free.

26: A SINGLE GRAIN OF SAND

Power is usually defined by what it does—its effects on people and places, positive or negative. But its effects aren't nearly as important as its sources. That's where you'll find the enduring mysteries . . . and the ultimate power.

Rhita Gawr's eye fell on Basilgarrad, its fiery red glow searing the darkness. Still stroking Marnya's lifeless body with the tip of his wing, the grieving dragon had not budged from the swampy pool.

"You," boomed the towering warrior, "will be the first to die." He took a heavy stride, slamming down his foot in the swamp. "The first of many!"

His roving red eye glanced at the dangling trail of black sparks that rose up into the sky. That, he knew, was all that remained of the dark thread that had delivered his power from the Otherworld; the rest of the cord had finally disintegrated. For the first time since he had arrived in Avalon and taken a troll's mortal form, Rhita Gawr's mouth twisted in a savage grin. His time, at last, had arrived.

He took another giant stride toward Basilgarrad. The force of his footstep shook the whole marsh, making the cowering ghouls burrow themselves deeper into the mud. Clods of peat and muck splattered the green dragon's back. Yet he still didn't move from Marnya's side.

Not far away, across the pool where Marnya had fallen, Ganta's small body shivered in fear at the hulking troll. But he didn't flee. Through chattering teeth, he vowed to himself, "As long as master Basil stays . . . I'll stay, too."

Glowering down at Basilgarrad, Rhita Gawr declared, "If you are too cowardly to fight me, I will simply crush you, like the worthless insect you are. And then I will do that to your world."

He raised his enormous foot, preparing to smash it down with all his weight on the dragon's back. His lips curling into a snarl, he spat, "You are nothing to me. Nothing! To me, you are as puny as a grain of sand."

Something about those words nudged Basilgarrad, stirring him from his grief. As the troll's words echoed around the Marsh, they also echoed inside his head. *As puny as a grain of sand . . . grain of sand . . . grain of . . .*

"Sand," said the dragon. He shook himself, as if awakening from a nightmare. Then he glanced over at Marnya, whose azure blue eyes he'd never see again. He cringed, rattling his wings against his sides. Yet now, for the first time since her terrible fall, he remembered *why* she had fought. Why she had died. For Avalon, the world they both loved.

The troll's monstrous foot rose right above him. But Basilgarrad paid no attention. He was too busy trying to remember something about sand—something that Dagda had once told him. How did it go? Yes, that was it! "Just as the smallest grain of sand can tilt a scale, the weight of one person's will can lift an entire world."

An entire world. In a flash, he thought about Dagda's strange command that he swallow one small particle—a single grain of sand, a drop of water, a wisp of cloud—from every realm of his world. He often wondered why the great spirit had given him such a pointless order. After all, what could he possibly gain from a single grain of sand?

His dragon's chest heaved as he drew a great breath. All at once, he understood! By swallowing a tiny particle of each place, he took into himself more than a portion of that place's physical marvels. More than that, much more, he took into himself a portion of its *magic*.

Rhita Gawr smirked, holding his massive foot over the dragon's back. Roaring louder than ever, he began, "AND NOW . . ."

Basilgarrad's eyes widened. Not because of the nearness of his own death—but because of what Dagda's command truly meant. His mind racing, he realized that if he held the magic of Avalon's realms, then he truly held the magic of *Avalon*. All of it. Every last glimmer. And that, surely, was the ultimate magic.

As Merlin had once told him, "You *are* Avalon."

"YOU . . . ," continued Rhita Gawr, his foot poised.

Urgently, with all his heart, Basilgarrad called to that magic. *Loyal friends of Avalon, wherever you are, hear me! Give me your power, your passion, your love of this world. Give it to me now!*

"SHALL . . . ," boomed Rhita Gawr, savoring this final instant before he killed the insignificant pest beneath him.

Basilgarrad felt a subtle, prickling sensation, somewhere deep inside his chest. It felt as if a tiny spark had been kindled. Then came another. Another. And another. Soon his whole body was almost buzzing with this new energy.

Right away, he knew its source. He could see glimpses in his mind, one after another, of tens, hundreds, thousands of creatures in faraway places—all across Avalon—responding to his call. Sylphs in Y Swylarna paused in midflight to send him their magic. Mudmakers in the farthest reaches of Malóch turned their huge brown eyes in his direction. In faraway El Urien, faeries hovered in a forest glade, their silver wings humming *Wings of Peace*. In Lastrael, the realm of eternal night, a small black butterfly glowed eerily, sending him a dark kind of light.

And more, as well. Brilliant fish leaped out of the Rainbow Seas of Brynchilla, their bodies shimmering like living prisms. All across Olanabram, giants slammed their huge hammers against mountains of stone, while farmers rang their magical bells. Deep in Rahnawyn's caverns of flaming jewels, a young dwarf played her harp, making musical fire that burned ever so bright. And even beyond Avalon, in the shimmering mist of Fincayra, a wandering wind stirred at his call.

"DIE!" roared Rhita Gawr, slamming down his foot.

Basilgarrad instantly rolled to the side, moving with incredible speed. He whipped his mighty tail and smashed it against the troll's descending foot—so hard that Rhita Gawr bellowed in pain. Seeing the troll wobble precariously on the other foot, Basilgarrad leaped into the air. Pumping his wide wings, he flew straight at the leg still planted in the Marsh and crashed into the troll's knee with explosive force.

Howling with rage and agony, Rhita Gawr teetered on his battered knee. One more bash against that knee from Basilgarrad's shoulder—and the troll shrieked, spun his arms wildly to regain his balance, and then fell with a shattering thud into the swamp.

Mud and peat sprayed in all directions. Even before all the clumps had fallen back into the bog, Basilgarrad arrived, hovering in the air just above the troll's head. He arched his back and curled his tail, preparing to strike a final blow to the red eye. He started to swing—

Slam! Rhita Gawr's enormous fist smashed into his chest. The dragon tumbled from the sky, rolling across the swamp. Finally, he skidded to a stop, covered in ooze and debris.

Basilgarrad, sprawled on his back, shook the heavy mud from his wings. He started to roll over so he could take to the air again. At that instant, a gigantic hand clamped down on one wing, pinning it to the ground.

Rhita Gawr's eye blazed with fury, just above the dragon. Hunched on all fours, the troll slid closer. His hand never moved from Basilgarrad's wing, and even the dragon's newfound strength wasn't enough to budge under so much weight.

"This time," vowed the troll, "you will die." Rivers of saliva ran over his lips and splattered the ground. "Most painfully!"

Desperately, Basilgarrad struggled to free himself. He slammed his tail, rocking the swamp. He twisted and tugged. But nothing worked. He couldn't escape!

Evil eye aglow, Rhita Gawr raised his other hand high into the air. Up and down his arm, immense muscles tensed as he closed his hand into a deadly fist. He started to bring it down—when a powerful gust of air, as forceful as twenty gales combined, suddenly blew his whole arm backward.

The gust expanded, sweeping through the Haunted Marsh. It moved so swiftly, with such great force, that it blew aside the heavy fumes that had for so long shrouded the swamp. In the time it took Basilgarrad to blink in astonishment, the entire marsh opened to the full light of the stars.

"Treachery!" roared Rhita Gawr, rearing backward. His lone eye squinted as he tried to adjust to this sudden burst of brightness. All around him, meanwhile, the marsh ghouls squealed in fright, dropped any prey they had been clutching, and scattered with the howling wind.

Basilgarrad seized the opportunity to escape. He wriggled free from the troll's hand, flipped over, and leaped high into the air. Before the half-blinded troll knew what was happening, the dragon had soared into position. Just as Rhita Gawr stopped squinting, Basilgarrad uncoiled his tail and slammed it down with all his strength into the evil eye.

"Aaaiiieeeee!" shrieked the troll. Then, with a moan, he fell over into the bog with a bone-crunching thud. Merlin and Krystallus, who were standing nearby, leaped out of the way—

barely avoiding being crushed beneath a huge, limp hand. Like a hillside of utter darkness, the body lay motionless.

The troll's eye, open to the sky, swiftly lost its red glow. In the very last instant before it extinguished, a thin, snakelike ribbon of darkness slithered out from its edge. The serpentine form slid along the ground, dodging the fetid pools, racing toward the place where the cord's last remaining sparks dangled down from the sky.

Merlin, picking himself up from the muck, was the first to see the dark snake. "Stop it!" he shouted, pointing with his staff. "Don't let it escape!"

Basilgarrad swerved in midair and flew after it. But before he could try to snatch it with his claws, the snake reached the rope of black sparks. It leaped onto the sizzling line and shot upward, zipping toward the empty gash on high.

Merlin swung his fist through the air. "Ogres' entrails!" he cursed. "Now we're sure to hear from Rhita Gawr again someday."

Krystallus stepped over to his father, clomping through the muck. He draped a mud-splattered arm across the elder's equally muddy shoulders. "Not for a very long time. By then, it might be your descendant—a grandchild, perhaps—who will have to deal with the situation."

The wizard stiffened in surprise and his eyes opened to their widest. "Grandchild?" he asked. "Really?"

Krystallus, almost grinning, shrugged his shoulders. "Who knows?"

Meanwhile, Basilgarrad swooped low, gliding across the

Marsh. His sensitive nostrils delighted in the smell of fresh air that now moved through this forsaken bog. No longer was the air choked by nothing but rancid pools and decaying flesh. Now, the wind carried many other aromas—the dry desert dunes, the hint of faraway forests, even the taste of mountain glaciers.

Plus one more thing. The wind that brought all those new aromas—the same wind that had blown so fiercely, allowing Basilgarrad to escape death—also carried another smell. The sweet aroma of cinnamon.

"Thank you, Aylah." Basilgarrad spread his wings to their widest, floating on the softest breeze he'd ever known. "I have missed you."

Currents swirled around him, filling the air with the smell of cinnamon. "You are hhhwelcome, my little hhh-wanderer."

The dragon's eyes brightened, glowing like emeralds. "It's been a long time since I've been called that name."

"Ahhh, yes," the wind sister replied, gently buffeting his wings. "But you hhhwill alhhhways be that to me, as long as the hhhwinds may blohhhw."

"You heard my call, and that is a gift." He glanced down at the swamp, where Marnya's lifeless body lay amidst the dead stalks of grass. "I only wish," he said with a sigh, "that every friendship could last as long as ours."

Aylah swept over his snout, a river of air that flowed across his scales. "And nohhhw, my little hhhwanderer, I have one more gift for you."

"What?" he asked, still gazing with longing at Marnya.

"Somehhhwhere dohhhwn there, softer than the softest hhhwind . . ." She swept closer, caressing the hair that lined his ears. "I hear a heartbeat. Ahhh, yes, the heartbeat of a hhhwater dragon."

27: PATTERNS

Whether it's cause for sorrow or joy, the turns you least expect are the ones you most remember.

A heartbeat?" roared Basilgarrad, his voice booming across the sky. "You hear a heartbeat?"

"Ahhh, yes," answered Aylah, sweeping through the gap of his missing tooth, which made the sound of a long, airy whistle. "Hhhwhy don't you try to hear it yourself?"

The great green dragon needed no encouragement. He had already whirled in the air, flapped his wings with all his might, and dived toward Marnya. She lay amid a cluster of dead marsh grass, as still as one of the faded brown stalks.

Basilgarrad landed, sliding through the muck and pools of the swamp. Foul-smelling ooze sprayed his snout, his ears, and even his eyes. But he barely noticed. *Could she . . . ?* he wondered. *Could she really be alive?*

He stopped within a claw's length of her body. Quickly, he crept closer, oblivious to Ganta, who sat in the rushes nearby. The young dragon, whose orange scales were thickly crusted with mud, watched solemnly as Basilgarrad lowered his head and placed an ear against her back.

He listened, trying to hear the slightest stirring of life. Beneath her scales, if Aylah was right, Marnya's heart might yet be pulsing—just as his own heart now pulsed with hope.

He heard absolutely nothing.

Reaching over with his wing, he pressed its tip on her back and pushed hard. Her limp body rocked, squelching in the mud. Again he lowered his ear and listened. Again he heard nothing.

He tried another push. Then another. And then another.

Still no response. Over in the rushes, Ganta sighed and turned away.

Basilgarrad's snout drooped, so that his nose touched Marnya's. "I have no more magic," he said quietly, his voice so soft it might have belonged to a purring cat. "I gave it all away, every bit, for Avalon."

His huge eyes blinked, brushing away the mist that blurred his vision. "But if I had any magic left, even if it was the only thing that kept me alive, I would give it to you."

For a long moment, he stayed there, as motionless as Marnya. Then he slowly lifted his head, which felt heavier than ever before. Aylah had been wrong—and, foolish beast that he was, he'd allowed himself to believe her! He snorted with dismay. He should have known, by now, having seen so many losses and borne so much suffering, that a wish alone could not change what was real.

Yet he had, for a moment, hoped it could. With all his heart.

Glancing one last time at Marnya, he turned slowly aside.

That was when he noticed, for the first time, Ganta. Their eyes met, one pair much smaller but glowing no less intensely; one pair larger in both size and experience.

"So . . . sorry," said Ganta glumly. He ground his tiny teeth together, then added, "At least you won the battle."

Basilgarrad peered down at him, unblinking. "And lost," he said with sadness, "the one person I most wanted to win it for."

A slight sound, more subtle than the rustle of a sparrow's wings, stirred the air. Instantly, the great dragon stiffened, from the tips of his ears down to the enormous knob of his tail. For he knew that sound.

The flutter of a dragon's eyelashes.

He turned instantly to Marnya, just in time to see her sapphire eyes open and look into his own. Held by that gaze, neither of them moved for several seconds. At last, she drew a halting breath. Awkwardly, she tried to shift her outstretched flippers and released a pained groan. Her right flipper seemed glued to the mud, unable to move.

Suddenly aware of what was happening, Ganta shrieked in surprise. He spun around in a circle, slapped himself with his wings, then breathed a spurt of orange flames.

Basilgarrad, meanwhile, stayed completely focused on Marnya. "Don't try to move," he counseled, still staring at her as if he'd never seen anything so marvelous. "I'll take care of you."

"You already have." Marnya slowly lifted her head. She started to say something else—when she caught sight of the mountainous corpse of the troll, sprawled on the Marsh. Her nostrils flared angrily.

"Yes," declared Basilgarrad, answering her unspoken question. "He's dead."

Her gaze, once more, met his. "You did it," she said breathily. "You saved Avalon!"

Slowly, he shook his massive head. "No, my love. *We* did it. All of us—every creature in our world who cared enough to help." His rumbling voice lowered. "No one person alone could have done it."

She smiled, understanding fully.

"Hoooooeeeee!" shouted Ganta. Raising his head to the wide open sky, he breathed another flicker of fire. Then, spying Merlin and Krystallus striding toward them across the bog, he jubilantly cried, "She's alive! Marnya's alive!"

When Krystallus shot his father a questioning glance, Merlin replied, "Basil's lady. A most courageous dragon. And, I should add, a good bit prettier than her father, Bendegeit."

"Bendegeit?" Krystallus shook his mane astonished. "A water dragon? Here? But how?"

"She flew, of course," answered the wizard nonchalantly. "Why do you look so surprised? This is, after all, Avalon."

Krystallus immediately broke into a run toward the dragons, almost losing his boots in the sticky muck. Merlin, clutching his staff, hobbled as fast as he could behind. His resident owl, though, couldn't wait. With a triumphant screech, Euclid burst out of the wizard's tangled beard and climbed into the sky.

As Basilgarrad and Marnya watched, their heads leaning against each other, the owl flew in a frenzy of geometric patterns. Euclid's path made a square, a trio of circles, then a jagged row of pinnacle-topped triangles. Then, with a loud clack of his beak, he launched into a maze of interlocking octagons.

"Something tells me he's happy," said the green dragon dryly.

Marnya's ears swiveled playfully. "Why, I wonder?"

While Euclid drew his designs upon the sky, Krystallus arrived. The whole of his face seemed to beam as he strode up to the dragons. Placing his hand on Basilgarrad's claw, he stared at Marnya in amazement. To no one in particular, he muttered, "This is, after all, Avalon."

Basilgarrad raised his head and gave Marnya a wink. "I think he's happy, too."

"As am I," said Merlin, puffing as he joined them. "As am I."

The wizard peered up into the huge green eye of Basilgarrad. *Very happy, indeed,* he said telepathically. *For you, my old friend . . . and for us all.*

"About what?" replied the dragon, trying his best to sound casual.

"Oh," answered Merlin with a twinkle, "nothing, really. Just Euclid there." He pointed the top of his staff toward the owl, who was making his most complex pattern yet. "You see, I've never known him to do anything so intricate. Look there! I think it's a dodecahedron."

"Really?" asked Basilgarrad, crinkling his brow in doubt. "It looks to me more like a wild-eyed old wizard."

Ganta laughed, spurting fire. Krystallus laughed, too, even as he gave his father a nudge. And so did Merlin, chuckling mirthfully. Marnya joined in, though she never took her eyes off Basilgarrad.

No one, though, laughed harder than the great green dragon himself. His voice carried across the Marsh, borne on the swirling wind that filled the air with the scent of cinnamon.

28: THREE GIFTS

You are expecting something wise, pithy, and dragonlike? Well, sorry to say, I'm all out of wisdom—if I ever had any. All I have now . . . is gratitude.

I have something for you."

Merlin nodded at his son, emphasizing the point. He ran a hand through the tangled gray hair of his beard, taking care to avoid the spot where Euclid was currently napping. "A gift. Actually, three gifts."

Krystallus, who was seated across from him on a rough boulder of rose quartz, cocked his head in surprise. He peered at the elder wizard—a man he'd known since birth, but whom, it seemed, he'd truly met only recently. "What sort of gifts?"

Merlin didn't reply. He merely nestled himself deeper into the gap between two burly roots at the base of an ancient beech tree. The tree's trunk tilted at a perfect angle to allow him to rest his back; a low branch draped in an ideal position for him to hang his hat and also prop his staff. Beech leaves, hanging near his head, trembled in the breeze, as if they were eagerly fanning his face. In every way, the tree seemed to be welcoming this particular guest. In fact, if Krystallus hadn't known better, he would have been sure that those massive roots had lifted and curled when his father sat down, just to shape themselves into a more comfortable seat.

"Oh, nothing special," answered Merlin at last, with a wave of his hand. "Just a few small trinkets to remember me by, since I'm leaving soon for Earth."

Krystallus started. "You are? Again?"

"Looks that way," said the wizard in a casual tone. "It seems that whole Camelot idea is proving a bit more compli-cated than my young friend Arthur had imagined. Time to look in on him."

The younger man nodded, swishing his white locks against his shoulders. "So how long do you expect to be gone?"

Merlin's brow wrinkled. "A good while," he said slowly. "Perhaps . . . forever."

Drawing a deep breath, Krystallus leaned back on the boulder. "I see."

"You seem a bit . . ." Merlin paused, clearing his throat. "Disappointed."

"Well, I was just starting to get used to having you around."

"I see," replied his father, twirling a few hairs on his beard. "That brings me back to those gifts."

"Nothing special, you said."

"Right. Although one of them . . . is a map." The wiz-ard's dark eyes gleamed. "A rather unusual map."

Despite his disappointment, Krystallus leaned forward on the boulder, suddenly curious. Aside from Serella, he loved nothing better than a new map. For him, it was much more than a piece of paper that described a possible journey. It was, in truth, a kind of journey itself—a way to bring a whole new place, maybe even a magical place, to life.

"So," pressed Krystallus, "what is this map you mentioned?"

"Right now, it's just a scrap."

"What?"

"A scrap." Merlin reached into a pocket of his robe and pulled out a small shred of paper, singed by fire around its edges. "But you know," he said softly, "it could become something more. Just as," he added with a quick glance at his son, "a small scrap of relationship, torn and burned by time, can become something more."

Holding the scrap in the palm of his hand, he showed it to Krystallus. "Recognize it?"

The younger man left the boulder to come closer. He studied the charred fragment in the old man's hand, all the while shaking his head. "All I see is part of what looks like an arrow. But there's nothing—"

He caught himself. Bending lower, he gently touched the burned edge. "Is this what's left of . . ."

"Yes," answered Merlin. "The magical map you gave to Basil. And if he were here right now, instead of flying around somewhere with Marnya, he'd be a bit surprised. He saved this scrap, you see, to show me how much you had done—and sacrificed—to help Avalon. And he saw me toss it aside on the battlefield. But I don't think he saw me pick it up again before we left."

Shifting his gaze to meet his father's, Krystallus asked, "Just why did you pick it up again?"

"Oh," answered the wizard with a shrug, "I suppose I was feeling just a bit . . . sentimental. For maps, of course."

Krystallus almost grinned. "Of course."

"And now," said Merlin, "let's see what it can still do."

"But it can only work once. I was told, quite clearly, that's the rule."

"Splendid! It's much more fun to be the exception, not the rule." With that, the wizard raised his other hand and held it just above the open palm. Concentrating his energy on the scrap, he intoned:

> *Arise, expand, be all you can be:*
> *Egg into eagle,*
> *Seed into tree.*
> *Dreams make real, elements own—*
> *Truth revealed,*
> *Flower full grown.*

The small fragment trembled, as if it had been touched by the same breeze that was stirring the beech tree's leaves. Yet this particular breeze seemed to swell steadily between Merlin's hands. The scrap floated upward, bent, and started shaking. Soon, a rich golden mist emanated from its edges. The piece of paper started to stretch along one edge, then another. It continued to expand, growing swiftly, until at last it reached its original size. Then, all at once, the mist seeped back into the surface, sizzling ever so slightly.

Surveying the newly restored square of paper, Merlin nodded and withdrew his upper hand. Like Krystallus, he gazed in wonder at the blank sheet, knowing that it held marvelous magic. With a final tilt of his head, he issued a silent command, and the sheet instantly folded itself into one-eighth its size.

"There," pronounced the wizard. "Your map."

He handed it to Krystallus, who took it gladly. After holding it in his own palm for a few seconds, the explorer slid it into his tunic—the same pocket that also held his starward compass.

"Will it still work only once?" he asked, gently patting the pocket.

"Only once," his father replied. "Unless, of course . . . we break the rules again." He winked. "But however you use it—be sure to use it well."

"That I will." Krystallus clenched his jaw with determination. "This map will help me find a route up through the Great Tree—all the way to the stars."

Merlin's bushy brows lifted, like fluffy clouds rising up his forehead. "The stars? That's a long way."

"Yes, it is." The explorer's eyes seemed alight. "And I'm going to get there, as I've always dreamed."

"You're sure? It could be dangerous to climb that high, without a pair of wings as strong as Basil's. Or a staff as powerful as this one." He ran one finger along the shaft that was leaning against the branch. "I only ask out of concern for your safety, lad. As your . . ."

He paused, not because the next word was difficult to say. Or awkward in any way. No, he paused just because he wanted to say it with so much honesty and gratitude.

"Father."

Krystallus smiled. "Thanks. But yes, I'm sure." Seeing the old man's uncertainty, he explained, "Look now, it's already the Year of Avalon 694. And no one—except for you, of course—has ever ventured higher in the Tree than the root-realms. There's so much more up there to explore!"

Merlin stroked his hairy chin. "Is this the time, though? Why now?"

"Why not? The long war is over. A new era has begun! You said so yourself, when we gathered for the peace treaty. Remember? You practically shouted, 'This is a new age— when our Tree, our home, will be blessed by a marvelous ripening.'"

"I said that?" The elder gazed up into the beech leaves over his head. "Not bad, really."

"Right," agreed Krystallus. "Already, people are calling this the Age of Ripening. Even that secret enchantress, the Lady of the Lake, used that term when she wrote her letter to everyone in Avalon. She went on to call this 'Merlin's greatest gift—a time of great discoveries as well as great perils.'"

"Did she?" Merlin's eyes seemed to dance with secrets. "What a nice thing for her to say." Then he added, perhaps a bit too gruffly, "Whoever she is."

"And I," vowed Krystallus, "am going to make some of those discoveries myself." He lowered his face to his father's, so that their noses nearly touched. "On my way to the stars."

"All right, then. I can recognize, in your face, that absolute determination to do something crazy." The corners of his mouth turned upward. "After all, you inherited it from your father."

Krystallus, pleased as well as amused, nodded. "I'm glad you understand."

Gently, the wizard patted the smooth bark of the beech tree, as if he were saying thanks to a friend. Then, grabbing his staff, he stood up. His eyes probed his son's face. "I do understand you, lad. And applaud you."

He cleared his throat. "Which reminds me of your second gift. Something that will, I hope, help you in your explorations."

Merlin turned his gaze to his staff. Squeezing just above its runes, he said quietly, "All right, Ohnyalei."

The runes, then the whole wooden shaft, started to glow with deep green light. While holding the staff with one hand, Merlin grasped it with his other hand—but this time his fingers sank *inside* the wood itself. The old man's fingers disappeared, followed by his hand, his wrist, and most of his forearm.

Krystallus watched, thoroughly amazed. He could only gape as his father reached deep into the staff as if it were a magical box.

Finally, the wizard announced, "There you are! Hiding from me, were you? Such a rascal."

He grunted, hauling back his arm. When his hand, at last, returned from the magical depths of the staff, it held a tall wooden pole with an oily rag around its top. Except for the strange silvery sheen that glittered on the rag, it seemed unremarkable, no different from other objects of its kind.

"A torch?"

"Yes, my son. To light your way."

Merlin passed the torch to Krystallus. The instant the younger man grasped it, the torch burst into flame. Vigorously it burned, radiating a steady, bright light.

Krystallus gazed at the torch, then turned to his father. A different kind of light seemed to shine from his face, mixing with the glow of the torch. "Thank you."

Merlin gave him a nod. "It will burn, I promise, for as long as you live." He swallowed. "As will my love for you."

The younger man stepped closer. "I think I know what is your third gift."

"You do?"

"Yes. And I have the same gift for you." He took another step toward his father, raised his arms, and wrapped them around the old man's shoulders.

Merlin, too, raised his arms. They encircled his son, sharing the embrace.

29: New Light

Sometimes the longest journey is only a beginning.

Time to fly!" bellowed Basilgarrad, calling to the sky, the root-realms, and the whole expanse of the Great Tree of Avalon.

Just as he'd done so many times over the years, he spoke those words as he began a new journey. This time, though, he said them with extra feeling—and dragonlike volume, loud enough to shatter the stillness for hundreds of leagues around. For his world, Avalon, was finally saved from the terrors of Doomraga and Rhita Gawr; his mate, Marnya, was deeply devoted to their life together; and his friend, Merlin, was firmly perched atop his head at that very moment.

The dragon beat his mighty wings, bearing Merlin higher. Each powerful stroke blew a great rush of air across the dragon's face, whistling past his radiant green scales and straightening the long whiskers that lined his snout. That same wind blew the wizard's robe so that it flapped constantly, but not as much as his beard, which twisted and shook so violently that Euclid finally jumped out and buried himself in a deep pocket. Meanwhile, Basilgarrad's wings continued to pump, carrying them upward, while his claws groped at the sky as if he were climbing an endless stairway.

Which, in truth, he was. This was no ordinary journey from one realm to another, no quick hop to the Rainbow Seas—where Marnya was even now cruising the cliffs to find the perfect spot for their lair. This was a journey far bigger, bolder, and grander. Something no mortal creature other than Merlin had ever done before.

Basilgarrad was flying all the way to the stars.

"Excellent, Basil," coaxed his passenger. He stopped stroking the hairs that lined the dragon's ear. "See there, those ridges? That's the lower reaches of the trunk itself."

Working his wings, the great green dragon changed the angle of his head so that he could see better what Merlin was describing. Sure enough, through the layered wisps of clouds, he caught glimpses of rough, vertical ridges. Dark brown, they rose upward in parallel rows, climbing into the thick ceiling of mist that swirled far above. Yet despite how high those ridges seemed to reach, he knew they were only the bottommost part of the trunk.

Higher they flew, and higher, plunging into the misty ceiling. For several wingbeats, moist vapors surrounded them, swirling so close that huge droplets formed on Basilgarrad's nose and eyelashes. The wind from his beating wings constantly blew those droplets backward, sending them splashing into his eyes or rolling down the full length of his enormous jaw. So wet was the air of those clouds that he thought, *I could be swimming, not flying*.

Keep swimming, old friend, counseled the wizard in reply.

Starlight burst over them, flooding them with light even as the bath of vapors abruptly ended. Slamming his wings against the shredding mist, Basilgarrad climbed upward, leaving behind the thick layer of clouds.

"Well done, old chap." Merlin tapped the back of the dragon's ear. "Now look there!"

Basilgarrad gasped at the sight. Blinking away the last of the mist, he peered at the new vista.

Just above them, rimmed with starlight, lay a maze of twisted brown appendages. Like immense fingers that stretched across the sky, the appendages seemed to be reaching for the stars. And in fact they were—for these were the branches of the Great Tree.

"So many of them," said the dragon, panting as he climbed.

"And each one is so big," added Merlin. "As big as an entire realm."

"The branch realms of Avalon," said Basilgarrad, his voice tinged with wonder. "All of them unexplored."

"Except, of course, by the creatures who live there. Creatures whom Krystallus will meet someday."

The wizard lifted the seam of a pocket in his robe to check on one particular creature who had decided to ride there. Immediately, he jerked back his hand, nearly losing a finger to an angry snap from Euclid's beak.

"Checking on the owl?" asked Basilgarrad, having heard the sound.

"Yes, and I'm glad to see that he hasn't lost his normal happy demeanor. Chipper as ever."

From inside the pocket came a vigorous burst of clacks and squawks.

Ever higher they flew, past branches after branches. When they passed close to the surface of one, Basilgarrad spied pinnacles dusted with snow, a canyon deeper than any he'd seen in the realms below, and several pits of bubbling fluid—resin, judging from the sharp, tangy smell.

"Good place, that, to gaze at the stars," said Merlin as they climbed past a flattened twig that faced the sky.

Through the twisting boughs they flew, over rumpled ridges, dense forests of unfamiliar trees, and starlit streams beyond count. Sometimes, Basilgarrad spotted constellations he recognized, glittering through the mesh of branches: He saw Pegasus, the winged steed; the twin circles of stars called the Mysteries; and the great arching line of stars that bards had named the Tail of Basilgarrad. More often, though, he saw new patterns of stars, arranged in shapes that bore no names at all—at least none that he'd ever heard in the lower realms.

One constellation, in particular, often caught his attention. Not because of its striking presence, but because of its even more striking absence. The Wizard's Staff, once so brilliant it had guided generations of travelers, lay completely dark. No sign of its seven stars remained, only a black gash in the otherwise radiant sky.

That, however, was soon to change. If Merlin had his way.

For the wizard's goal in this journey—his last before going to the distant world called Earth—was to relight those very stars. With a little help, of course, from his favorite dragon.

With every beat of his wide wings, Basilgarrad lifted them higher. Though the air grew thinner, making each beat more difficult, he persisted, ignoring the aching muscles in his shoulders and back. Glancing below, he glimpsed a shimmering rainbow through the shredded clouds. Was that, perhaps, the watery realm where he and Marnya would make their home? Where a child, part blue water dragon and part green élanodragon, might someday be born?

The only root-realm he clearly recognized from above was Stoneroot, which often showed between the gaps in the branches. *Aha!* he thought. *Now I know why it's the brightest of all the realms, a question I asked Aylah so many years ago.*

"Because it catches the most light through the branches," commented Merlin matter-of-factly. "Just as Shadowroot gets the least."

"Since you know everything," grumbled the dragon, "how much higher do we need to go?"

"Not much, old chap. We're almost there now."

Basilgarrad's shoulders tensed as he flapped his wings again and again. Starlight glinted on his scales, making them glow like living constellations. Stars flamed nearer than ever, shining with a light that was both physical and spiritual, as much the essence of fire as the wellspring of dreams. A rippling line of light shimmered above them, cutting across the center of the sky: the River of Time. It divided, he remembered Merlin telling him, not just the stars but the two halves of time, past and future.

The stars grew more radiant with every wingbeat. Soon they flamed so strongly that Basilgarrad was forced to squint to dim the brilliance. He kept flapping, climbing higher and still higher. The dragon's wings felt heavier than ever, almost too much to lift.

"All right, Basil!" The mage's cry echoed within his ears. "Just hold us here, will you? All I need is a moment."

As the dragon pumped his wings, groaning from the strain, he glanced up at the dark gash in the sky. For the first time, he saw some variation in that place, seven thin circles that gleamed subtly in the blackness. Could those be the extinguished stars? And could they be more than what they seemed? Some sort of passageways, perhaps?

Merlin drew his staff from the loop in his belt. He grasped it with both hands, planted his feet firmly on the scales of the dragon's head, and raised the staff as high as he could. Pointing it toward the dark gash, he said one simple phrase.

"Bring back the light."

The staff released a brilliant flash of light. Its radiance filled the sky so intensely that many people all the way down in the root-realms witnessed the event. To the stargazing bard Inglo, it was a luminous eruption that seemed like an exploding star. To the dark elves of Shadowroot, the sudden flash illuminated their entire realm for a brief instant, causing their oversized eyes to sting for many days afterward. And to

Marnya, the flash revealed the silhouette of a powerful dragon against the glowing sky.

When the flash faded, Merlin lowered his staff. Above his head, seven stars blazed bright once more. Satisfied, he tapped Basilgarrad's ear.

"Thanks, old friend. Our work is done." Then, so quietly that the dragon almost couldn't hear, he said, "Except for one final task."

30: A SMALL REQUEST

Sometimes people will ask a friend to do what they would never ask an enemy.

W hat task is that?" asked Basilgarrad, his voice booming across the heavens.

Without waiting for Merlin to answer, he tilted his wings, making them shimmer in the light of the rekindled stars. Slowly, he started to glide downward. His glistening green body floated like an enormous kite through the interwoven branches of the Great Tree—only in this case, the kite's tail was the mighty, undulating tail of a dragon.

"It's not so much a task, Basil, as a request." The wizard's beard fluttered in the wind, glowing as if it were really a silvery flame that had sprouted from his chin. "A small request."

"Hmmm," said Basilgarrad. His enormous eyes opened to their widest. "Now I'm nervous."

"No need," answered Merlin, a bit too quickly. "After all, you are the greatest dragon of all time!" He raised his voice, expounding on the theme. "Wings of Peace, you are justly called. The unrivalled victor at the Battle of the Withered Spring. The hero of the Battle of Fires Unending. And the only person, aside from Dagda and myself, who has ever defeated the immortal warlord Rhita Gawr."

The dragon's brow furrowed, lifting the scales under the wizard's feet. "Now, after all that praise, I'm *very* nervous. You want something difficult, that's certain."

Ignoring the comment, Merlin continued to expound. "Not only that, Basil, you are the true embodiment of our world. The magic and history of Avalon, all rolled into one." He nodded. "And also," he added more softly, "the best friend any wizard could have."

Basilgarrad lifted a jagged wing, sending them coasting between two branches covered with greenery. Smells wafted up to him, tickling his sensitive nostrils. Some of them reminded him of aromas he recognized—walnut shells, ripe lemons, and the musty scent of fresh deer prints. Many, though, he'd never encountered before—a mixture of woodland mushrooms and rising bread, a type of feathers that might have been coated with olive oil, a pungent root that mingled turnip and something more like an ogre's breath.

As they glided downward, the dragon grumbled, "Whatever it is, I can tell it's going to hurt."

"Really?" Merlin wrapped his arm around the huge ear by his side. "What makes you think that?"

"Because," replied Basilgarrad, "I know you well."

The old mage gave a sigh. "Too well. You're right, my friend."

Shifting his wings, the dragon glided over a branch whose surface held hundreds and hundreds of luminous lakes. So clear and still were these pools that they reflected the light perfectly, as if they had swallowed the stars themselves.

"Tell me, then," he pressed. He moved his ear, giving the wizard a nudge. "What is this small request?"

"Well . . ." Merlin paused to take a deep breath. "It's just that . . ."

"Yes?"

"I want you," said Merlin at last, "to make one more sacrifice. The greatest sacrifice of all."

"What?" Basilgarrad's throat vibrated with a loud rumble. "You want me to stay away from Marnya?"

"No, no. Not that."

The dragon shook his head as he glided lower, skimming past the vertical ridges of the great trunk. "That's good, because I would never agree to it. Never."

"I assure you," said the wizard, "you won't have to leave Marnya. You can even stay with her in that new lair of yours. At least until the time comes for you to . . . well, to do something else."

Basilgarrad flapped his wings, guiding them over a mountain that rose from an especially burly branch. Its summit shone with fresh snow. He glanced down at a herd of strange three-horned beasts that galloped across a white ridge, so similar to—and yet so different from—the elk he'd often seen running through the high peaks of Stoneroot.

"So tell me," he asked, "what is this sacrifice?"

"You're not going to like it."

"I know that already!"

"Well, Basil . . ." Merlin cleared his throat. "I want you to become . . . *small again.*"

"What?" roared the dragon, so loud his voice echoed among the branches of the Great Tree. "You want me to *what?*"

"Become small again," the wizard replied, his own voice sounding meek and small by comparison.

"No!" bellowed Basilgarrad. He spun a complete loop in the air, nearly dislodging his passenger. "Why in the name of Avalon would you want me to do that?"

"Because," answered Merlin while clinging tightly to the dragon's ear, "if you become small again, that would be the ultimate disguise. You can wait in hiding."

"Wait for *what?*" Branches seemed to rock from the force of the shout.

"For Rhita Gawr! He will return someday, I'm sure of that. And he will try, once again, to conquer Avalon."

A deep, angry rumble came from the dragon's throat.

"But if," the wizard continued, "he doesn't hear anything for years about you—the great green dragon who defeated him—he will conclude you are dead. And he will grow careless and assume that you no longer threaten his plans."

Merlin leaned into the dragon's ear and whispered excitedly, "That's when you can foil him! You see, I have foreseen that I will have a true heir, a brave lass or lad who will try to stop Rhita Gawr. But that young person will need your help to prevail."

"Never," declared Basilgarrad. "I do not hide from anyone. I do not wait in disguise. And most of all, I do *not* want to be small. No, never again!"

"But Basil," the wizard protested, "it won't be forever. Just . . . a few centuries."

"Centuries!" bellowed the dragon. "Not only do you want me to give up my size, but to live that way for hundreds of years?"

"Only a few hundred," said Merlin meekly.

"No! Without question, no."

"Won't you even consider—"

"No." The dragon shook his head for emphasis, which knocked Merlin to his knees. "Absolutely no!"

Slowly, the wizard stood again. Supporting himself against the dragon's ear, he pleaded, "The entire fate of Avalon will hang in the balance."

"No."

"My heir will need to be carried to the stars, just as you have carried me."

"No."

"You will face Rhita Gawr again in combat. It will be, I predict, the greatest battle in Avalon's history. And it will happen not on the land, but in the sky. It will be a battle that will shake the stars."

Basilgarrad didn't respond. He merely stretched his wings to their widest and glided downward, circling over the branch realms. Wind flowed across his face, whistling through the gap in his teeth. At last, the corners of his gigantic mouth lifted in a terrible grin.

"Combat?" he asked. "Me against Rhita Gawr?"

"Right," answered Merlin, nodding eagerly.

"The entire fate of Avalon will hang in the balance?"

"Right again."

"The chances of success?"

"Very low, I'm afraid."

"And the risk of death?"

"Very high, I'm afraid."

"Then," declared Basilgarrad with a thunderous roar, "I shall do it."

"Really?" Merlin practically skipped on the dragon's scales, he was so relieved.

"Yes," agreed Basilgarrad, nodding his enormous head. "For if I win, Avalon will continue to thrive. And if I lose . . . that would be a death truly worthy of a dragon."

Merlin stroked the soft hair that lined the dragon's ear. "My friend," he declared, "you are even bigger than your great body."

Basilgarrad roared in agreement. And his roar echoed from the root-realms all the way to the stars.

EPILOGUE

The older I get, the more I enjoy a new day, a new friend, and best of all, a new adventure.

More than three centuries later, in the Year of Avalon 1002, a tiny lizard sat in the crack of a rocky ledge. A breeze blew over him, ruffling his cupped ears and batlike wings. In his little eyes, a strange green fire glowed. For he could see, at long last, the young person he'd been waiting for all these years, striding toward him on the grassy trail.

As the person neared, the tiny creature's eyes flashed brightly. From the excitement of what he knew was to come. And also from the certainty of where he wanted to go after this adventure ended: to a cavernous lair in the cliffs overlooking the Rainbow Seas. There he would find a certain water dragon whose radiant blue eyes he knew well. She was waiting for him in that place, along with a feisty young dragon with turquoise scales.

He unfolded his wings slowly—as if he were not just a tiny, zany-looking lizard but a glorious, powerful dragon. Then he announced, his voice thin but determined:

"All right. It's time to fly."